Neon Hemlock Press
www.neonhemlock.com
@neonhemlock

The Dead Withheld
L. D. Lewis

Cover Illustration by Shan Bennion
Interior Illustration by Shan Bennion
Interior Design and Layout by dave ring
Edited by dave ring

Print ISBN-13: 978-1-966503-07-1
Ebook ISBN-13: 978-1-966503-08-8

L. D. Lewis
THE DEAD WITHHELD
Neon Hemlock Press

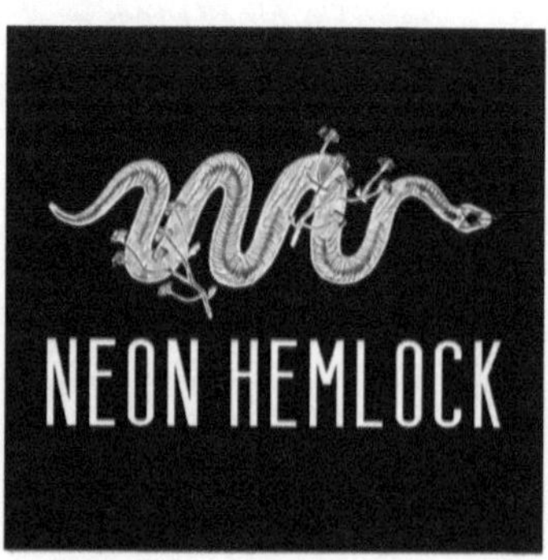

NEON HEMLOCK

the dead withheld

L. D. LEWIS

IZZY CARTER TEETERED on her barstool. It was
less because she was six fingers into this fifth of
bourbon and the world was on a tilt, and more
because its uneven legs stuck in the crumbling brick of
the alley's ancient walkways. This was Mark Street, a
string of pocket bars and taquerias set up in the mouths
of candy-painted shipping containers and strewn with
lantern lights kinder to bloodshot eyes. It catered to people
who preferred the dark to San Guin's nighttime neon hell,
people without a fear of mayhem or the uncanny magics
that made up their expanded reality.

She slugged down the last vestiges of liquor and refilled
her glass, trying to make it an even ten fingers instead of six.

The owner, N, cut and lit a cigar behind the bar and flipped to a news screen she watched on mute. N was a leathery old woman with large eyes and a gravel scratched voice who also sold bootleg brujeria supplies to rich tourists and their terrible children. Her shelves were dotted with human eyes and rattlesnake tails and likely her own backwash suspended in artisanal glass bottles of grain alcohol. And if she didn't like you, she'd swear on your god (never hers) that they were potent in their spiritual properties and worth every cent you had on you at the time.

N made a good living.

Dizzy stuck with the bourbon.

She moved her glass from where her phone vibrated testily against it and instead watched raindrops alight on the invisible heads and shoulders of the dead milling among the oblivious living. The long wall of the noodle shop behind them was caked with bright graffiti, tithes of the all-seeing Color Man's disciples. Between the rain and the swimming of the liquor in her blood, the colors danced in Dizzy's vision arrhythmically to the bass bumping in the noodle house.

It was late on a Friday (or early on a Saturday, she'd have to look at her phone to know) and she could do with a moment left alone. But still, her phone vibrated. Any other profession, these would have been her off-hours.

Deadwalkers existed for centuries as lone witches, scattered throughout the world and held sacred as messengers of the dead to the living. Dizzy Carter was one of them but little was sacred anymore. Fewer folks knew that about her than knew she sang the blues; even that was little more than a poorly kept secret.

Six years ago she'd been in love and on the verge of more. More attention, better gigs. A career worthy of the life she shared with Lonnie Baxter. Then the Fallen Angels serial killer dropped the love of her life off the roof of their apartment building.

Dreams of that night forced themselves on her when she was either too exhausted or not stoned enough. She was a private investigator now, and well aware of the cliche. The calls she ignored were undoubtedly from clients, people searching for cheating spouses or blackmail fodder on people they owed money. The police had long since halted the search for the Fallen Angels Killer. On quiet Friday nights in the dim glow of N's paper lanterns, Dizzy considered she should as well. After all, not even the dead could find Lonnie Baxter.

A silhouette shrouded in raindrops approached the bar and stood beside Dizzy.

"Evening, friend," she greeted the dead patron in respect. The words slid from her numbing mouth. She wasn't in a state to hear them speak back.

A chill breeze cut the humid alley air and Dizzy plied the hood of her jacket before deciding home would be warmer. She polished off her drink and reached across the bar for another short glass into which she poured a slug of bourbon—an offering—for the invisible guest before rapping her goodbye to N and pressing a gold coin on the bar top by way of a tip.

Her first steps were trickier than she thought they'd be, poorly measured and on no certain path. She looked around to measure her drunkenness by the steps and ramblings of other patrons on the strip and paused as a face disappeared between two bodies at a street vendor's stall. Despite herself, her heart skipped and she squinted trying to find some magical way to peer between raindrops.

Lonnie?

Lonnie's face appeared again, closer. She was smiling, great almond eyes cut to glimmering half moons and lips moving in excited, silent speech as she walked closer. But she was translucent, little more than a bright shadow in an old band t-shirt against the bodies moving behind her. She wasn't a ghost. This was a memory.

Dizzy stayed riveted to the spot as the memory of Lonnie approached and then passed her in the alley. And then she matched Lonnie's steps as they headed to the street, desperate to remember this moment in their past, to hear her voice match the words she mouthed and the laughter in them.

They walked for blocks, well past the place Dizzy was living now. She remained unfazed as strangers clipped her shoulder walking the other direction and immune to their curses when she walked into them. She drifted through crosswalks shunning crowds with their umbrellas and the onslaught of car horns. If she stayed beside Lonnie's walking form, she could catch her eye, feel the wonder of being seen by her again. She knew better than to reach for Lonnie's hand, to try and touch her or she may disappear.

Rain and neon light from the signage of nightlife crashed through Lonnie and threatened to obscure her completely until she stopped on the sidewalk on a calmer street. They stood before a wrought-iron screen backlit in warm sunset-orange light. For full seconds, Lonnie looked into Dizzy's eyes, a smile playing on her lips.

"I miss you," Dizzy whispered. "Can you hear me?"

The memory of Lonnie kept smiling and appeared to burst into laughter, pointing at something well over their heads across the street. Instinctively, Dizzy turned to look at what was only a billboard of lights, advertising Heating Co. Power and Light. She remembered this part of the memory. On this day, it had been the movie poster for Lonnie's first major performance, a throwback noir flick called Tiger Moon.

Dizzy remembered this next part, too, when the excited memory of Lonnie raised her hands to the sides of Dizzy's face and kissed her. She closed her eyes in hopes she might feel it. When she opened them, the memory was gone. And Dizzy, as she'd always been, was alone.

2

5HE WAS CENTER-STAGE under searing light at the Crane Lounge, a bougie spot known for its gold leaf cocktails and backroom gangland symposiums. They usually liked their doll-faced, moody darlings on piano in the dark but there she was bathed in gold, all hoodoo and gutter blues and a little lipstick. The room was packed with San Guin's upper-crust citizens entranced with the magic of her voice. Cherries of expensive cigars dotted a sea of brown faces under hazy blue lights. They toasted with brown liquor and clapped and swayed to her rhythm in their seats.

And then her B string snapped. The chandelier lights flickered. The crowd froze as if time had stopped and all their eyes—their impossibly wide, glowing eyes—were on her.

The music still played in her head. She kept singing. People scattered throughout the audience began to vibrate. Three of them. Ten. Twenty-one. She was terrified. The buzz became deafening and then she blinked and they were gone and all was silent. The audience, the stage crew, the bartenders, the waitstaff. All gone except for a woman in a white dress at the bar with her back to her.

Dizzy fled the stage as a new pitch grew in her ears. She crossed the dining room to the bar in the back and the pitch grew louder until it was clearly discernible as a scream. Filled with dread, she reached out and touched the woman's shoulder. Lonnie turned to face her. It was always Lonnie. Her eyes were white like the dead always were. And when she went to smile, Dizzy caught the puckering of knots in the corners of her sewn-shut mouth. Then Lonnie kissed her and filled her head with her scream until she felt like she was falling and...

Dizzy's eyes flew open and immediately took in the listless ceiling fan and pink-amber morning of a bedroom. It wasn't much of a view, but sunlight filtered through patterned curtains and wooden blinds and the windows along the wall were open to let in new air and early traffic sounds of the city. Her gun, two aspirin, and a glass of water waited on the bedside table.

This was Carmen's place. She ran the Rising Sun, a bordello of exquisite and highly skilled spies, sirens, and succubi. Its success proved that some men would volunteer their lives for an orgasm rumored to be worth it.

She reached, but the bed was empty beside her. The plum-colored sheets were barely rumpled but Carmen's scent lingered there on her pillow. Dizzy swung her feet over the edge of the bed and waited for her equilibrium to right itself.

"Morning," Carmen called from the bathroom.

"Hey." Dizzy grimaced, tasting her own breath. She downed the aspirin and dug her phone from the pocket of her jeans on the floor to begin swiping through her notifications. Four missed calls. It was Saturday. At least she'd only slept the night this time.

"You alright? You look like shit."

"Long night. We can't all wake up looking like goddesses."

"You're right." Carmen smiled into the mirror. "You sticking around long enough to eat something?"

"Nah, I need to get going. I've been slacking on this case."

Carmen turned to face her in the doorway. She was impossibly beautiful, full and soft in her curves and the pout of her lips. Her eyes were round, brown, and disarming, but in the right sunlight the pupils flickered to slits and golden scales shimmered just below the surface of her perfect brown skin. She was a demon, after all. Sometimes it felt rude not to be in love with her.

"Oh yeah? New lead on Lonnie?" she asked.

Dizzy shook her head, trying to forget the Tiger Moon billboard, the memory on the street. There hadn't been a lead in years.

"Then I'll rephrase. You're sticking around long enough to eat *something*."

Dizzy was both hungry and in no mood to argue. "You're the boss."

Satisfied, Carmen sauntered over and kissed her. Dizzy was immune to the soul-stealing drain inflicted on men. She let the nerves in her lips tingle with Carmen's venom and inhaled the heady fruit scent of her. "Brush your teeth," Carmen winked. "See you downstairs."

The door clicked shut behind her and Dizzy stared through the windows a moment longer at the faded billboards and outed neon signs of sleeping nightlife hotspots. She'd found herself here in this room with this view more often than she expected. She'd started work as a PI a few years ago, when looking for Lonnie's murderer became a financially unsustainable obsession. She'd found the bordello contained a wealth of information and they found her story sweet enough to give it to her. The relationship with Carmen herself had gradually become more personal but short of love.

They understood each other's positions perfectly well. The tormented Dizzy was emotionally unavailable and Carmen hadn't the energy to waste bringing her out of it. Still, they enjoyed each other's company.

Her phone vibrated. She didn't recognize the number so she shimmied into her jeans and boots while she waited for it to go to voicemail. The untied laces whipped the dark hardwood floor as she made her way to the bathroom.

She sighed at herself in the mirror. Her brown and heavily freckled face was lacking lately in its glow. Her lips were pale and parched. Last night's eyeliner smudged itself into an unkempt ring around her eyes and she'd sweat out the gel keeping the edges of her hair in line. At least she'd had the sense to gather it into an ombre pineapple on top of her head before passing out in Carmen's bed.

She docked her phone in the mirror console. Three green dots blinked in the mirror before the home screen's at-a-glance information organized itself along its edges. *Weather and Traffic brought to you by Heating Co. Power and Light. Eighty-eight degrees and sunny. Accident on the expressway, tack 30-minutes onto your commute.*

"Read new messages," Dizzy commanded before running the tap cold and splashing the water on her face. A transcript of her newest voicemail appeared and scrolled up the mirror.

NEW MESSAGES
09:14 - MISS CARTER THIS IS CAROL UNDERWOOD. ROGER HAS BEEN GONE FOUR DAYS NOW. YOU AGREED TO HELP ME BUT YOU TOO ARE MISSING. WHERE ARE YOU? I NEED TO KNOW IF THE BASTARD IS DEAD OR JUST GONE.

Ah, Mrs. Underwood. Dizzy shook her head. She wasn't lying when she said she was behind on a case but this wasn't her first creeping husband assignment. All she had to do was rule out Mr. Underwood being dead.

The missed calls log read all the same numbers since last night. Mrs. Underwood had been persistent.

"Desert weather," Dizzy said, and a weather map on the mirror revealed a stormfront rolling in from the east. It would be over San Guin around nightfall. She had time.

She managed to wrangle her curls into a neat-enough braid, then scrubbed the taste of morning and bourbon and caapi cigarettes from her mouth. Deadwalkers relied on certain herbs to maintain their connections to the dead world and the blended cigarettes she used had stained a black spot inside her bottom lip where they'd rested over the years. She poked at the spot. Her stomach growled. She collected her phone and the gun from the bedside table and headed downstairs.

The Rising Sun was six floors of violet-painted hallways, a dozen rooms each with gold doors. The interior of the elevator Dizzy rode down was painted in baroque tapestries of intermingling kings and conquered warriors and the lascivious demons who owned them; a bit on-the-nose, but exactly this clientele's kink. The elevator stopped on most of the floors and the men who'd survived the night stepped anxiously inside. They appeared wasting away inside yesterday's suits, their gazes vapid and distant, looking through Dizzy and the men beside them. By contrast, the sirens who accompanied them on the ride down were radiant and made up in every variation of perfect. They allowed the weaker men to lean on them and kept conversation to make sure their clients didn't pass out in the elevator.

"Hiya, Dizz," they'd wink at her.

"Hey darlin'," she'd reply.

She followed the vixens and their overnight clients to the bar nook across the posh lobby. A line of colorful, sweet-smelling elixirs in shot glasses lined the countertop and each man took one. Their color returned in a wave along with the spark in their eyes. The little brews would keep them vital at least until their next visit.

And there would be a next visit. Some stayed for coffee or fruit and small plates of cooked things. Their sense of self restored, they carried on as if this were a normal morning they were spending with a normal mistress before heading off for their work day. Eventually, they would waste away altogether, and the sirens would devour their bones for the marrow.

Dizzy took a seat at the bar where Carmen flirted and made stiffer drinks for the master of the universe types in tailored suits who didn't begin or end a day without a finger or two of top-shelf booze. Carmen was an experience they insisted they were meant to have. They had to settle for her laugh and a few precious moments of witty banter. Dizzy admired the regality she had about her.

"You made it," Carmen said, turning to Dizzy. "Coffee?"

"Whiskey and a water," Dizzy replied. "I gotta take the edge off this thing."

"You sure you know the difference?" Carmen winked. She'd started pouring the whiskey before Dizzy even asked and slid the glasses over in front of her. "What's the case you're behind on?"

"Missing husband," Dizzy said with mocking enthusiasm. "The wife's on my ass. But to be fair, it's been four days."

"Four days? He dead?"

"Don't know. I need to make a trip to the desert."

A girl appeared through the kitchen doors bearing a plate and Carmen gestured with her head that whatever was on it was Dizzy's. Chorizo, rice, and a fried egg. Dizzy dug in and then paused when she noticed Carmen was still standing over her.

"You're seriously going to watch me eat?"

"Yes and you're not getting up until it's gone. I'm serious. Death's one of those things I do here and you look like I've been working on you."

A succubus named Ash joined Carmen behind the bar. She was a leggy dark-skinned girl with wide, brown eyes and a beatific smile. Her face lit up when she saw Dizzy.

"Dizzy Carter!" She leaned over the bar to kiss her cheeks. "You're never around this long."

"I was commanded," Dizzy replied.

A hulking giant of a man she recognized appeared a few seats down and leaned on the bar, waiting for a drink. He had a heavy, brooding brow and about a day's worth of beard on his stony face. Tattoos covering scars Dizzy'd put there the first time they met peeked above the collar of his work shirt. He tapped a crushed box of clove cigarettes on the bar.

"Tomás. Howzit?" Carmen smiled at him.

"Carmen. Carter." He nodded at the women but avoided Dizzy's eyes.

"Tommy," Dizzy muttered.

Ash served him. He thanked her and slugged his drink and ducked out of the building with a cigarette between his lips. Dizzy watched him go.

"So tell me what you've been up to?" Ash insisted. Her lips and the lids of her eyes were painted gold and nearly distracted from the faint scales beneath her skin as the sun angled through the front windows. "Any progress on Lonnie's murder?"

"Not for a while. Not unless you've got news for me." Dizzy hid her grimace behind a mouthful of rice. "Not even the dead can find Lonnie Baxter."

"I think it's romantic you're still trying," Ash mused.

"And stupid," Carmen added with a piteous smile as she poured herself a drink. "I understand love. Human love. *Eternal* love. But walker or not, Desdemona, the living ain't supposed to spend this much time with the dead." Carmen clinked Dizzy's glass with her own then turned to Ash.

"Make sure she eats," she added pointedly and moved away to tend the clients.

Ash let out a long, low whistle. "Was that a lovers' quarrel?"

"I don't know what that was." Dizzy stared after her, hoping, dreading, their relationship hadn't just turned a corner. She changed the subject. "You've been working Tommy for what? Three years now? How is he not dead yet?"

"Five. I think he's protected."

"By what? Craft? I didn't think Tommy got down like that." Dizzy watched him through the glass front windows.

"I don't know. This fell out of his pocket." Ash turned a black card over in her hand. An emblem like the bones of outstretched wings was etched into a corner. Ash handed it to her.

"Hotel key card?" Dizzy suggested, even though years of tracking cheating spouses and secret drug habits had familiarized her with every hotel in San Guin. This was no key card. But it was familiar...

"Not likely. He's got a brand that matches it on his chest."

"You ain't ask him what it meant?"

Ash shrugged. "His money's good. That's brujo business."

Dizzy's phone vibrated. Mrs. Underwood's number.

"Damn it." She slugged the rest of her whiskey and stood up. "I have to go."

"Want me to apologize to Carmen for you?"

Dizzy thought a moment about whether or not she'd actually done anything requiring an apology. "Just tell her I'll see her later."

She grabbed a few bottles of water from the elixir table and headed out into the sun.

Her car was a gift from Lonnie. It was black and impossible to keep clean with the desert dust that attached itself to everything here; modeled after one of those vintage bad boys that sounded like a lion when you turned the engine over. They called them muscle cars over a century ago. Loud, environmentally irresponsible.

Powerful. A fitting relic of the Former United States. She'd swapped out for a better fuel system, sure, but no one could drive a stick anymore so it was hard to steal.

She donned her sunglasses and tried not to think about Carmen as she carved her way out of the city east into the desert. Towering, congested architecture overflowed with massive billboards and signage in muted colors. Almost everything here was styled to be most alluring at night. Glimpses of back streets revealed pop-up marketplaces and people seeking refuge in the shade. Bustling city streets finally gave way to small, even dustier homes, garages, and trading posts. An old, defunct gas station marked the forty mile point beyond the city limits where all the rest was brush and rocks and unforgivable dry heat.

Dizzy's loose curls whipped in the wind and her fingers mocked the plucking of guitar sounds on her radio. She hadn't lost the music. She simply didn't love it the way she used to. She'd given it up to investigate Lonnie's death and the Fallen Angels Killer in ways the San Guin police wouldn't, combing the vice-riddled other-life of San Guin and threatening the dead for answers. The drinking habit that sustained her sleep now was far from the worst thing she'd done in the name of vengeance. Before going to the dead for guidance, she'd taken lives of her own.

And kept them.

She was a dangerous, reckless witch.

About the 66 mile marker she turned south off the paved road and took to the dirt. Dizzy's tire tracks weren't exactly well-worn into a trail, but she'd been out here enough to know where she was going. She stopped twelve miles clear of the main road and before a rocky eye formation of an arching land bridge joining two mesas. No one who wasn't looking for it would notice the fifty-foot circle of spiraling stones on the ground here. Their surfaces were marked forever in her own bloody fingerprints but the desert wind had covered them in a layer of dust.

Dizzy grabbed a small brush from her glovebox and got out. The sky darkened and storm clouds were collecting just over the horizon through the eye but the scent of rain wasn't carrying this far on the wind just yet. It took an hour, but she made her way around the circle, brushing off each rock until her prints were once again visible. And then she went to her trunk for a wooden bowl into which she poured the bottles of water and placed it in the center of the circle. Water was life and her offering. The dead would see her as long as the water was there.

She sat on the hood of her car to collect herself, to leave Carmen and her nightmare here on the edge of the circle before lighting a caapi cigarette. The smoke she exhaled as she muttered the start of her incantations streamed into the air over the circle, impervious to the wind. She walked the outer ring, still praying, still chanting, tapping ash over the stones until it stopped hitting the ground and joined the gathering fog. Caapi was a troubling thing. Maintaining lucidity was always a challenge by the end of the third lap. She was not so much exhaling the smoke anymore as it was being drawn from her and the chants became commands for the dead to take no more than what was theirs. Her breath was her own and she had not come to give it to them.

The stones began to bleed in vein-like jags over the sand until a perfectly circular pool formed. She fought the parts of her mind that told her snakes and scorpions were being summoned here, that the sky had turned black and the sun had cracked open and was dripping its gold onto the mesas. The fog of caapi smoke and ash solidified into an orb before she closed her eyes.

"You again."

Dizzy opened her eyes to find the sky was blue, the day was hot and breezy. Everything was normal, right down to the familiar skeletal visage of Nico, one of her regular informants, standing on the edge of the circle before her.

He'd been buried out here maybe ten years ago, a mob casualty like countless other bodies, and any spirit to take her call took it in the form of his body. His living eyes were white and his skin still clung to his frame in places but the rest of him had wasted away. The bowl of water in the circle began to steam.

"Me again," she replied. The cells of her body felt like soda bubbles, fizzing and popping as the caapi worked to keep her tethered to the living world.

"You come to pay what you owe?"

Dizzy ignored the question. "I need a little help with a case."

Nico held out a hand kept together by more magic than tendons. Dizzy tugged a cigarette from its case, handed it over and lit it for him. He had no lungs. He barely had lips, so she imagined this affectation was more a creature comfort.

"What's the case?"

"Missing husband," she said, pulling up a picture of the dapper Mr. Roger Underwood on her phone. "Underwood. Disappeared about four days ago."

"Well the wife ain't a widow. The dead don't know him. Not unless he's pulled a Lonnie Baxter," said Nico. He waved the cigarette in loops for its dancing smoke.

Dizzy bit her tongue to keep from saying something stupid and cut her eyes at him from behind her mirrored sunglasses. At least she could tell Carol for sure that her husband was running out on her again.

"So when do you plan to settle up?"

"I haven't found the Fallen Angels Killer yet." Dizzy frowned and looked southward toward nothing.

"It's been six years."

"I know how long it's been," she snapped. "Time is a real thing on this side."

"Hey, I'm just the messenger, girl. You've owed the dead them three goons you got stashed for a long time.

They clearly ain't doing you no good so I would *suggest* you turn them over before the dead come looking."

"Yeah alright." Dizzy fidgeted.

"That it?" Nico asked, picking at the crumbling collar of his dingy purple shirt.

"Yeah, that's it." She sighed and leaned back against the car. Something in her back pocket settled wrong against the metal. She pulled out the black card Ash had given her. "Friend of mine showed me this. It looks familiar but I can't place it. She says it's brujo business."

Nico took it from her, inspected it, and handed it back. "What's it to you?"

"A dangerous man was carrying it and has the same symbol branded on his chest."

"Yeah?" The flesh of Nico's remaining cheek went up in a smirk. "You sure the demon shit keeps just finding you and you're not going looking for it?"

Dizzy sighed frustration at the sky. "No, I promise it keeps finding me." She'd had a run-in some years ago with a familiar demon, but it'd been personal, on behalf of her mother and not something she'd considered a bigger deal if she resolved the issue by killing and maybe robbing him a little.

Nico sucked his teeth, not buying it for a second. "Either way, looks like San Guin's got a demon problem. And not them girls you hang around, either. Your buddy with the brand can tell you more about who it is and why they're here though. We don't know that."

"A demon problem?" Dizzy muttered to herself. She ran her fingers over the symbol on the card, racking her brain for where she'd last seen it.

When Nico chuckled, it sounded like three voices at once. "Don't do it."

"Don't do what?"

"I know you like to dabble but demons are not your thing.

You don't do nothing in moderation and this is just something new to obsess over. That's not your world."

"Look, I just asked you what it was."

"Ain't none of us new here." Nico flicked the caapi roach toward the water boiling away behind him. "You will pull this thread and kill or be killed by whatever's at the end of it. And if you die, we'll never be rid of you."

"Alright, Nico." Dizzy rolled her eyes as the sound of the last of the water began to sizzle out.

"Stay in your lane, Dizzy Carter."

"*Bye* Nico."

He tipped a hat he didn't have and turned back to the circle just before his bones settled to dust again and were swallowed up by the earth.

Dizzy threw her bowl back into the trunk and the deadwalker fatigue settled heavily in her bones. She sat in her car, drumming the card against her steering wheel.

In the beginning, her investigations had lacked a certain professionalism. There'd been a year of blind and reckless rage. A handful of brass-knuckled back-alley brawls with San Guin's goons and lesser gangsters had translated into some gruesome interrogations. A few of these interrogations needed a change of venue or more time than the immediate circumstances permitted. And so she'd killed three men she knew knew *something* and kept their ghosts hostage beneath bell jars in her bedroom where she might find uses for them at her leisure.

Presumably, someone was doing the same thing to Lonnie and that was why the dead couldn't find her. The difference was they knew where to find Dizzy to collect their due.

Dark clouds billowed closer and the wind now brought the smell of rain with it. Staying in the desert after the sun went down or hid itself behind storms invited the dead to plague her for what was theirs and what they needed from her.

And not all of them behaved themselves. The living energy of the city diffused the dead too easily to harm her there, so she'd learned the hard way not to doze off in the desert in her post-caapi states.

She dialed the Rising Sun and threw the car into gear before skidding on the desert gravel headed back to the city.

"The Rising Sun, this is Sugar," said a voice befitting the name over the subtle din of entertaining in the background.

"Sugar, it's Dizzy. Is Ash around?"

"Oh hiya, Dizz. She's...no, I don't see her. She must be upstairs. You want Carmen instead?"

"No," Dizzy replied. She paused, guilt itching in her chest. Why was she avoiding Carmen? "Can you just have someone call me if Tommy shows up there? Today, tomorrow, whenever."

"He in trouble?"

"No, I just want to talk to him."

"Uh huh," Sugar chuckled. "I'll let Ash know."

"Thanks."

Almost as soon as her phone hit the leather of the seat beside her, it began to vibrate. Dizzy shook her head, cleared her throat, and answered it.

"Mrs. Underwood, hi. I have good news depending on how you look at it: Roger's not dead."

2

THE APARTMENT WAS *blue in the dark. The alarm system buzzed in silence until she punched in the code. Their combined birth years. She dropped her guitar case by the door and rifled through mail on the sideboard.*

A shadow moved in her periphery and footprints glowing green in some cacophonous dance pattern appeared on the hardwood floors.

She scanned the room to notice the slightest things amiss. An upturned corner of an area rug. The rumpled section of a bed she'd made perfectly this morning. Dizzy fit her footsteps to the marks on the floor to see if any sense of them could be made and they took her stumbling across the room to the open patio door. The city was black even under moonlight and the air was still.

And then she looked down.

Lonnie's eyes gazed emptily off to the side as her body was folded the wrong way over the downstairs neighbor's balcony railing. Dizzy screamed her name so loud the black buildings across the street began to crack and crumble. And then Lonnie's head turned and looked up at her. She said nothing, but pointed a red manicured finger toward the sky.

A feeling like electricity raised the fine hairs on her arms. She looked up into a shadow she didn't recognize, and then...

Thunder clapped and fat raindrops pelted her windows when Dizzy jolted awake alone in her apartment. The popping carbon sensation of her skin persisted, clear sign she was overexerting herself. She dragged a hand over her face to restore some sort of normal feeling there—smearing an errant tear on her cheek—and checked the time on her phone.

Barely five a.m. on a Monday morning. She'd lost the weekend. When not enough time was rested between communion with the dead, she lost time like this and her living self would continue on without her mind. The last thing she remembered was the slamming of her car door when she arrived home on Saturday, but take-out cartons and a half dozen empty Coke bottles strewn about the floor indicated she'd at least eaten since then.

She smelled coconut milk. Curry had been involved.

Her living self always managed to eat or brew coffee it never finished or break a plate it never cleaned up. But it never seemed capable of peeing for her so bounding across her bedroom to the bathroom was always the first most urgent thing she did when she woke.

She sat.

And went.

She washed her hands and checked the missed calls on her phone. Carmen had called three times and not left messages. Dizzy didn't call her back. Instead she ran the shower in hopes the heat would steam the gunk off her soul.

This apartment wasn't the one she'd shared with Lonnie. It was smaller and on the opposite end of the city. She lived on top of a bookstore in the set of rooms off an antechamber that acted as her office and foyer.

Outside her window it was still midnight-dark. Remnants of the city's nightlife crowd made their way from the side streets of pop-up black market shops and pocket bars toward the bodegas and noodle houses along the main road. The Thai carryout spot across the street was still popping beneath the turquoise neon of its sign. Blue light splashed the slick umbrellas passing beneath it and mingled with the head and tail-lights of folks headed home from third shift jobs. No one out for any other reason would be sober enough to drive at this hour.

She cracked the window to let in fresh air and headed back to the shower.

The ebony altar dusted in incense ashes and the iron ouroboros skeleton suspended before a bright sun tapestry on the wall behind it was hers. Apart from that and a locked cherry wood record cabinet containing those souls she'd stolen, most of the furniture had been Lonnie's. She tried to forget that. But it was impossible sometimes not to see a phantom of her sleeping body coiled perfectly in their patterned sheets piled high like junihitoe layers in lieu of a real blanket. The system of cubed shelves on the far wall were still filled with her books. Their pictures together and posters of Lonnie's movies were boxed up elsewhere.

When she got in, the running water still reminded her of every time Lonnie insisted she sing to her from their kitchen to take her mind off the dialogue she obsessively rehearsed with the showerhead.

Funny how I've stopped loving you...

She caught herself humming and stopped. That had been some other shower. She'd sung to her from a much nicer kitchen. And it was all such a long time ago.

She got out and dressed and braided down her wet hair before it dried itself into a chaos it'd be painful to sort later. The black card peeked out at her from the back pocket of Saturday's jeans she'd discarded in a heap on the floor.

When she met Tommy years ago, she'd been chasing down a lead in a jazz spot in South San Guin. Her mark made her and called Tommy—who worked in security at the time—to nab her in the alley while the mark made his escape. They fought. He was too big for her to kill easily. She was too quick. They left each other banged up and bloody, but alive.

She knew this card was trouble. She knew she and Tommy were never destined to be friends. Still, she plucked it up and turned it over in her hands before chucking it onto the bedside table. Was it familiar? Or was she just hoping it was?

She collected the accumulated food trash and deposited it in her tiny kitchen en route to her conference room (repurposed dining room) across the apartment. It was muggy behind the frosted glass doors that separated it from her office (a second-hand desk in her "living room"). She hadn't bothered with the space in a year, maybe more, who could tell. It housed all of her investigative materials—the conspiracy wall with its pins and photos, the stacks of musty cardboard boxes containing less interesting records and evidence—surrounding the Fallen Angels Killer. Paper, she'd determined, could be saved. Anything the cops gave her digital access to could be manipulated or destroyed. And would be, if they were involved, which—judging by how unsolved the case remained—was still a distinct possibility.

She scanned the items on the wall, looking for the symbol on the card. Drivers licenses, crime scene photos, maps, selfies, and webs of social circles. The killer terrorized San Guin over the course of an otherwise unremarkable summer.

They'd dropped eight victims from the tops of things throughout the city, each with their tongues cut out and their mouths sewn shut, a move next-to-no-one knew rendered the victims catatonic in the dead world.

Those of them who arrived.

There had been eight victims in all. Lonnie was the last.

Dizzy was numb by now to the grotesqueries of the victims' smashed and distorted bodies, the unnatural splay of limbs popped from their joints beneath swollen, bruised skin. The pictures of their living faces for comparison still seemed to hold secrets. Had she been around to sever the threads that bound their lips shut, maybe their ghosts could have whispered a name.

Nico mentioned demons, and that tracked. Most of the victims had fallen in places with no overhead structures. Too far into the middle of a road to have been thrown from high-rise windows like Kit Walker, or deep into the middle seats of an outdoor amphitheater like Nadege Colon. The killer would have had to be flying, but she'd checked with air traffic control. It wouldn't be ridiculous to consider they'd had wings, but not even the Dracs had those.

She found her gaze halted in the area of the wall bearing Nadege's materials. Gallery owner, age 38, objectively gorgeous, towering, dark-skinned, well-heeled, not well-known, but on the rise in her own way at the time.

Dizzy frowned. There was nothing on the wall with the symbol from the card, so she turned to the boxes on the table behind her to flick through the papers and photos she'd considered less than wall-worthy before. Buried within the stack was a candid photo used in a press release for the opening of her first gallery. Nadege was in a white suit, smiling and pointing at the camera, mid-sentence in a conversation with a beatific and apparently intrigued young man beside her. In her pointing hand, she held a glittering white clutch purse and what appeared to be the day's mail.

The angle wasn't straight-on, but Dizzy could see now what was clearly the symbol from the card emblazoned on the outermost envelope. The edges of it were feathered and brown as if burned or branded, but it was the same.

Her heart skipped. She slammed the photos onto the table and stalked back up the hallway to her bedroom closet. It was small and over-crowded with the things she couldn't bother placing. Amid the vintage milk crates of even more vintage vinyl records was a crate bearing Lonnie's paper things. Headshots, scripts, old mail, notebooks she'd collected more than used, to-do lists with things still undone.

She snapped off the rubberband that bound the final three days of Lonnie's mail together and was flipping rapidly through it when she made a sound, something like a yelp of both excitement and horror. A bill. A wedding invitation. And an open envelope with an odd wing insignia burned in its center. The envelope itself was empty.

She'd never paid attention to the burnt envelope in the stack of Lonnie's mail. It was only a flicker of a memory but she recalled the sensation of thumbing through the stack and barely registering the faint smell of burnt paper and thinking nothing of it. She'd been too excited for Lonnie to come home.

This is it, she thought, her hands trembling as she traced the symbol with her fingers. Well, not *it,* but it was something. Some mystery that tied Lonnie to at least one of the other victims. Maybe all of them. The longer she stared at the symbol, the more it appeared to be a shattered bird…or a broken body.

This was *something.*

She hadn't killed Tommy that night in the alley because she *thought* he was just doing his job. She could hardly fathom all the ways he would suffer if it turned out he had anything to do with what happened to Lonnie.

First thing's first, however. Her boot laces slapped at the baseboards as she stomped back to her conference room. She snapped a picture of the photo of Nadege and her friend and had her phone begin the work of identifying and potentially locating them. It pinged by the time she snatched her keys and gun from her bedroom.

Emmanuelle Tiva.

"Of the *Tiva*-Tivas, of course." She sighed, reading the screen. "Fuck."

Manny here was a Drac; descended of some really, *really* old world vampires in the natural, somebody-gave-birth-to-them kind of way and not the formerly-mortal-and-thus-inherently-possessed-of-an-exploitable-weakness kind of way.

"Well, good day to die I guess." Dizzy shook her head. She grabbed a set of brass knuckles with silver-tipped spikes from her bedside drawer, just in case. Silver bullets were fucking expensive.

DRACS WERE CONSIDERED royalty not out of any concept of material wealth, but in that they were the apex predator in whichever environment they desired to place themselves. Individually, they could be unassuming, but they lived in nests, surrounded by their own, and had a fungal sort of quality where the right tonal screech at the unhinging of their humanoid jaws could summon the entirety of their kin, from the most affluent to the most gutter-bound, all to descend upon an enemy. And they did not play about family.

Emmanuelle Tiva lived in a middling district—or at least his grandmother did. Dizzy tracked him from the wealthy center-city high rises he'd lived in back when Nadege was alive, to these perfectly quaint stucco townhomes along the western edge of San Guin.

Not even the dead milled about here. It was a curious thing to feel alone because of it. Still, she knew she was being watched when she knocked on the oxblood door of 661 Box Street. These were dinner hours but there were no food smells on the street. And though it was getting late, the HP&L street lamps here remained off. The one light she could see was just a flicker some blocks away. It told her how deep into the nest she was.

Her phone vibrated in her back pocket. Carmen. Dizzy sighed. Her thumb vacillated between the screen options to answer or hang up. She'd missed half a dozen calls from her already. She stowed it again without choosing when the door opened.

A young man—Latine, twenties, middling height, a bit bored in the eyes—stood before her. The air that rushed past him was definitely marked by death, along with spices and a little smoke. He didn't speak, but studied her.

"I'm looking for Emmanuelle Tiva," Dizzy offered.

The man frowned, nose twitching at the air around her. "What are you?"

"Me? I'm an investigator. Not of Emmanuelle, they didn't do anything. I'm here about Nadege Colon. I understand they were friends."

He said nothing for a few tense moments and Dizzy tried discreetly glancing over his shoulder to make sense of the dark behind him.

When he stepped aside, the path revealed not the interior of a home, but a dark alleyway. Dizzy hesitated to step inside, wondering if she'd been all that convincing, if Nadege's name was truly enough to ensure she was being welcomed in peace and not for dinner. Inevitably she steeled herself, shoving her hands into her jacket pockets and nodded by way of thanks before stepping past him.

It took time for her eyes to adjust once the door was closed behind her. But they were still outside. The roofline overhead ended abruptly and there was sky and only the

fuzzy light the moon provided. The Drac probably didn't
need much in the way of light. The man looked back as if
signaling for her to follow, a sheen marking his dark eyes
like a cat's in the night. The walls were lined with what
seemed to be apartment doors and there were sounds of
people living lives behind them. He rapped his knuckles
casually on two of them as they passed, someone emerging
from each to walk behind her until she was flanked. Dizzy
swallowed hard but kept her pace. This didn't seem the
place to exhibit fear.

The alleyway let out into a courtyard lit by a scant
number of eerie green lamps and whatever the moon
provided. The apartments extended upward two additional
floors and surrounded the square. Roots of a giant tree
raised the paving stones surrounding it. There was a small
garden, a dry fountain, and a few scattered stone tables
bookended by mismatched dining room chairs. The
doorman pulled one of these into a clearing where Dizzy
could be watched and pointed for her to sit in it.

She obliged and he disappeared, leaving the other two
guards behind her. She tried not to find the interminable
number of doors disorienting as people stepped out to lean
over railings and observe her. There would be no getting
out of here if she needed it. She regretted not answering
when Carmen called.

Someone's great-grandmother approached from behind
her, escorted by the doorman. She was short, maybe 5'2",
wrinkled and hunched, long fingers clutching the top of
a walking staff that clicked violently on the pavers. The
state of the silver bun at her crown indicated she'd put
it there that morning and hadn't bothered with its slow
unraveling since.

Undoubtedly the matriarch.

She stood at Dizzy's side, examining her. Dizzy was
unsure whether standing out of respect would be received
as a threat. She remained seated.

"I am Maia, Emmanuelle's grandmother," said the woman. "Desdemona Carter."

"What are you?"

"I told your doorman, I'm an investigator."

"No." Maia leaned forward and took a long, predatory inhale. "*What* are you?"

"I'm…human. A deadwalker." She hoped that was clear enough. Dizzy's business was with dead humans. The undead had nothing to fear from her. She hoped that meant a default to mutual respect.

"Hm," Maia grunted, unimpressed. "A drunk deadwalker. Bad for blood, you know. Smells like poison. The taste, though… eh." She trailed off into a chuckle that suggested she didn't mind it so much.

Dizzy cleared her throat. "Right, well, Emmanuelle was friends with this woman, Nadege Colon." She showed Maia the picture on her phone. "She was the fourth victim of a serial killer seven years ago. My wife was the eighth. If Emmanuelle can help me find who killed our girls, I would be incredibly grateful. It's the first lead I've had in years."

"Manny talked to the cops already," Maia said, unblinking.

"Well, since when has that helped anyone?" Dizzy shrugged.

Maia did not move for a long time. And then she signaled almost imperceptibly, and in Dizzy's periphery a number of people moved. One came to draw out a chair in front of Dizzy and help Maia to sit in it. Two more disappeared behind a set of doors on a wall near the courtyard entrance.

"You know it's bold of you to come here," Maia told her with an incandescent toothy grin. Her hands bore down on the engraved walking stick between her legs as her assistant cut and lit a cigar for her. Dizzy noted the old woman's tattooed knuckles and more ink peeking above the collar of her housecoat.

"I do. I appreciate your time," Dizzy replied.

Maia's expression turned somber as she exhaled an impossible cloud of thick pumpkin-tinged smoke. "When she died, it destroyed my Manny. You will see. They were the very best friends."

A trio of people emerged from the courtyard doors; two helpers and an emaciated Emmanuelle between them stepped into the dim light of the space. Maia's helper placed a chair beside her and Maia, pat the seat of it to invite Emmanuelle to sit. They did sit, but stared into some middle space between the three of them. Dizzy found their face gaunt, the skin of it almost deathly pale and robbed of its rich goldenness from the photo. It made their eyes seem overlarge beneath the dark curls pouring around their face.

"Manny, this girl, she is helping find Nadgie's killer," Maia said.

At the mention of Nadege's name, Emmanuelle finally looked at Dizzy as if discovering her there for the first time. They looked like they'd been crying for ages and could pick it up again at any moment.

"I'm Dizzy Carter, Emmanuelle. I didn't know Nadege, but my wife was one of her killer's victims. I found this picture in the investigative notes. This symbol—" she enlarged the picture on her phone to examine the symbol on the envelope, "—matches this letter I found in Lonnie's mail. Do you know where Nadege got this letter? Who sent it?"

Manny seemed to ignore the letter and took Dizzy's phone to focus on Nadege's face in the picture. Their lip quivered and a haunting sort of wail began in their throat. It shook the air and Dizzy felt the fine hairs of her arms raise as figures on the balconies and edges of the square began to agitate. Maia covered Emmanuelle's hands with her own and growled lightly, stilling the activity around them. She then gently returned Dizzy's phone to her.

"Do you know the letter?" Maia asked them again.

Dizzy held up Lonnie's letter in case it helped.

Manny blinked repeatedly and inhaled a long time. "She was so excited," they whispered. "That day, that letter…we had just opened the gallery and she found a new artist. That letter…some grant or philanthropist, some investor. I don't know. I didn't know it would matter so I didn't…*save* it, I didn't remember…"

"Shhh…" Maia hushed them as their words began to tumble and roll together. "Okay. Okay," she soothed.

"You know, I found her." Manny snarled suddenly, their eyes boring into Dizzy. "I saw what they did. I can't stop seeing it."

"I know," Dizzy told them. "I found Lonnie."

"So then you know." Manny's voice broke. They leaned forward, reaching for Dizzy's hand. Maybe they'd never met a victim's loved one before. Maybe they never knew someone else knew this torture. "How could they do that to something…to someone so beautiful?"

Their intensity was increasing. Dizzy could feel her hand being crushed before Maia pulled them back.

"What else do you need?" Maia insisted, smoke billowing.

"Do you remember meeting any investors? Any suspicious strangers? Anyone with an infatuation maybe with Nadege?"

"No, no, no!" Manny was becoming increasingly distressed. . "I told you! I didn't know it would matter so I didn't keep it! I didn't keep the memories! I want them back I swear to you but I can't find them!"

Maia signaled her helpers again. "We lost Manny for some years to *the scene*, you know. To these drugs. It's why we bring them here away from the city. My baby wanted to lose memories then. They were only able to lose the wrong ones." She ashed the remainder of her spent cigar and pointed back at Dizzy. "You know that life, no?"

Dizzy nodded wordlessly, somehow embarrassed. She'd been without the woman who raised her for some time and thought she'd forgotten the ability to feel shame.

A light drizzle began to fall in the courtyard and the curious onlookers began to disappear behind their doors.

"I'll walk you out." Maia got to her feet by leaning on her staff, waving off her helpers. Dizzy walked alongside her through the corridor and back to the front door. By then the drizzle had become a steady downpour. "If you can fix this, if you can give Manny this justice, my family will be grateful." Maia opened the door for her. "And you will find you do not need the silver in your pocket."

Dizzy felt for the brass knuckles in her jacket pocket and smirked. "Can't be too careful."

"Lives short as yours, I agree." Maia smiled.

Dizzy stepped out into the rain. Porch lights turned on along her path to her car. A friendly gesture in the dark.

An investor had made a dream come true for Nadege. Had they also financed Lonnie's movie? What was Kit Walker's thing? Restaurateur? And what did it have to do with Tommy? A moneyed security client maybe? If that raggedy bitch knew somethi—

"Excuse me," called a chipper male voice as she unlocked her door. Dizzy startled. Back on the sidewalk, a short, sunburnt sort of bearded man dressed in white stood beneath a white umbrella.

"Yeah?" Dizzy called back.

"Forgive me, you just look *so* familiar," he said with a smile.

Dizzy shrugged. "One of those faces, I guess."

"Ah!" He yelped breathlessly. "You're the deadwalker!"

Dizzy frowned, confused and mounting suspicion. "Not *thee* deadwalker, there's more of—"

"No, you're the one," he interrupted. "Curious, though. There's no dead here. What brings you to this neighborhood?"

"Can I help you, stranger?" Dizzy made a show of the gun on her hip and her eyes swept the sidewalks and rooftops but there was nothing.

"Is that what you do? Help people?" He approached her at a saunter, wingtips clicking the sidewalk. "Do you find that when it matters most, you are…too late?"

"You ask *a lot* of fucking questions." She ripped the gun from its holster and raised it just as Maia's door opened and three of her family members emerged onto the stoop.

The man in white stopped, glancing over his shoulder at the apparent warning. "No matter," he smiled again. "I was just on my way elsewhere. Good to see you, Desdemona Carter, so up close. I'll give your regards to hell, shall I? Very popular among the demons. And you'll give my regards to Lonnie—" here he chuckled, "—whenever next you see her."

Dizzy pulled the trigger before a single question could properly form but the bullet stuck in the air between them and dropped to the gutter an inch before it could reach his nose. She walked closer, intent on unloading the clip, maybe just strangling him if she had to, but the Dracs grabbed her with surprising strength and disarmed her with even more surprising speed. She roared and fought against them until Maia reappeared in the doorway.

The man in white pointed at her and mouthed along, tauntingly as she looked pointedly at Dizzy and declared, "Not my house."

"Who are you?" Dizzy asked him. "Who the fuck are you and where is Lonnie?"

He put up his hands blamelessly to Maia and then proceeded to walk back up the sidewalk.

"Who are you! Who is he?" Dizzy turned to Maia and the men holding her. Before long she was allowed to jerk herself from their grasp, but the moment she took her eyes from his back, he was gone.

"Why did you stop me!" Dizzy shrieked as they gave her back her gun. "That was him! That was our answer!"

"Not him," Maia said sternly. "There are children here. Not. My. House."

"*Not him*," Dizzy repeated, incredulous. "What do you mean *not him?* Do you know who he is?"

Maia looked around to the others as if asking them the same question. Each shook their head.

Maia sighed. "No, we do not know him. But he did not bring a gun to my door. Go home. I am too old for regrets and would hate to take back my offer of friendship."

The three Dracs stood aside and allowed Dizzy back to her car. They waited in the street as she pulled off, screaming curses as she found her way back to the city lights. There was no man in white among the souls on the sidewalks.

# 5

BACK IN HER dining room, Dizzy pored over every picture of every victim, looking for other traces of the symbol, any sign of the man in white and found nothing. But Kit *had* just opened a restaurant, and Will Hadley had *just* conducted his first symphony not five days befo—

Her office (living room) doorbell buzzed. Indeed a brown silhouette hovered on just the other side of her frosted glass door. Dizzy glanced out the window. Barely daylight.

Too early for a client, she thought. *One of the tenants must have locked themselves out again.*

When she opened the door, however, she cursed silently.

"So you're alive," Carmen said with a raise of a perfectly arched eyebrow. She stood with her hands in the pockets of a black bomber jacket worn over a black t-shirt and black jeans and impossibly high black stilettos. Rain steamed off her so quickly she barely looked like she'd been wet in the first place.

Dizzy stood back to let her inside.

"I thought I might stumble on a body I'd have to drag out of here."

"Those your body-dragging shoes?" Dizzy asked.

"I can do anything in these shoes," Carmen said plainly.

Dizzy didn't doubt it. She led her into the kitchen where she poured them each a finger of bourbon like it wasn't six a.m.

"So what's going on?" Dizzy asked, sliding a glass along the counter. She leaned against the windowsill next to the fire escape and wondered if she might need to use it.

"I could ask you the same thing. You haven't been returning my calls."

"Yeah, I went to the desert on Saturday."

"That case took a lot out of you?"

"Something like that."

Carmen nodded slowly. "So it has nothing to do with you avoiding me?" She stared Dizzy down as she sipped from her glass.

Damn it.

"No…" Dizzy started, a heartbeat too late.

Carmen grinned and pointed a lacquered fingernail at her. "I knew it!"

"Carmen…"

"What is it? I'm meddling? Trying to tell you how to do your job? You think I'm coming for Lonnie's spot?"

"Look." Dizzy sighed. "I know we understand each other. Or we understood each other. But I'm not ready to complicate it. And maybe by now I should be. I don't know what Lonnie would do in my position. I can't just leave her lost because I can't guarantee that's how she would handle it. So if it's a problem…"

"Oh calm down." Carmen laughed and Dizzy thought the room seemed brighter for it. "It's already complicated. You think I want in on that whole possessive girlfriend mortal coil thing and I don't. I know you're going to do what you have to do. But I do care about you. Your life is short and I don't want you to spend the rest of it like this."

Dizzy didn't respond immediately, just nodded into her glass and shifted her weight, wondering about the proper etiquette of this situation. Carmen was first to fill the silence.

"Tommy came by Saturday night. He was pretty pissed off. Said Ash picked something out of his pocket."

Dizzy bristled. Tommy didn't have a problem hitting women. "She gave me a card she found on him. I have it." She led Carmen back to the bedroom where she dug the black card out of last night's jeans.

"Ash alright?" she asked.

"You know we handle ourselves." Carmen ran a thumb over the symbol and handed it back. "Hagenti."

"What?"

"It's an insignia for the Legions of Hagenti. Not the worst of the global gangs, I'd say, but that depends on which legion you run into."

"Nico said the demon would be a problem."

"Well who's commanded a legion of anything and not been a problem? I'll be the first to say things are weird here lately. There's…a balance shifting. Hell's taking more of an interest in the city than they used to. I think Gen got here first, got ahead of whatever's coming, but he won't be the last."

"*Gen?*" Dizzy raised an eyebrow.

"Don't be jealous; it's beneath you. Honestly he's very clever and a little eccentric. Fancies himself an art connoisseur and traffics in that and gold on the black market. Thinks it's highbrow human stuff," Carmen explained sardonically.

Dizzy bit her lip. Carmen was already watching her expectantly. May as well out with it.

"Come here." Dizzy led her back to the dining room and spread papers out across the table in an order that likely only made sense to her. "Lonnie had some mail with that symbol on it. I saw it the night I found her and I guess just…forgot *until* I saw the same piece of mail in the hand of victim number four." She pointed to the picture of Nadege and Emmanuelle. "This kid's a Drac. I went to talk to them last night…"

Carmen blinked rapidly.

"I know, I know. But look. Emmanuelle tells me this is from an investor or philanthropist or some shit. Nadege had just opened a gallery. Lonnie had just landed a movie. These people…all of them in some kind of creative field and on the verge of *something*. The Fallen Angels Killer was making dreams come true and then murdering the dreamers at the height of their happiness."

"That's…fucked up," Carmen replied.

"Where I'm stuck is cross-referencing all the investors I can find on their projects. There's a little overlap but almost everything's got a board of at least twelve people or…"

"Or they're angel investors." Carmen slid the card onto the table and tapped at the symbol. It did look like an angel. "Unnamed. Not findable."

"Shit." Dizzy ran a hand over her face.

Morning had come, though it was hard to tell with the storm. There was no sunlight peeking through blinds to paint things morning colors. But in the silence between them in her dining room, Dizzy recognized the roar of a garbage truck and the uptick in swishing noises as traffic picked up outside her window. She could tell Carmen was trying to decide if more information would help get her killed.

"Look, Gen is…old. I haven't seen him in at least a few centuries. He's unlikely to look the same, but he's almost certainly in a human form. One of the victims had to have talked to him, found nothing to raise an alarm. When you look for him, just know he's sober so you won't find him in the usual places. Might find the legion though. And he rolls around with this guy the Magician. Without him, Gen can't hold his human form."

"What's his other form?"

"A bull," Carmen said and finished her drink. "But with wings and a fucked up temper."

"Of course there's wings."

Carmen tapped her nose.

"This Magician…wear a lot of white?"

"Well it varies." Carmen shrugged. "They're mortal, so there've been many of them over time. Encounter with a very specific kind of weirdo?"

Dizzy couldn't bring herself to explain what had happened with the man in white without throwing up. She changed the subject. "You know where I can find Tommy? See if he'll tell me where to find the Magician?"

"Tommy…will not be back to the Sun anytime soon." Carmen sighed and sauntered over. "We couldn't kill him as long as he's got that mark but his little temper tantrum got him banned."

Dizzy nodded. It was of no consequence. She knew how she'd find him.

Carmen palmed the sides of her face with hot hands and kissed her. "You could be happy. You know that, right?"

Dizzy got to forget herself in the pools of Carmen's ancient eyes and felt what it would be like to breathe without the weight of Lonnie's life on her soul for fleeting moments before she pulled away. "Not yet."

"Famous last words of a lot of dying men." Carmen winked. "Do what you've got to do, but come see me soon. I don't want to have to come back here. Uninvited, anyway."

Dizzy agreed as she always did and walked her back to the front door. She waited at her bedroom window until Carmen got into her car parked on the street below before making herself another drink.

She unlocked the record cabinet with a key she kept on her altar. Three dolls, each on their own shelves, lay idle and unmoving beneath glass bell jars. They were more head than body, carved from the wood of elephant trees with black pits burned into their faces for over-large eyes and crude nicks in their torsos—*I, II, III*—to distinguish one from the other.

"Wakey wakey, boys," she whispered. Wisps of incense smoke that had created a haze in the room were drawn into the doll bodies to mimic breath until they twitched and began to stand. Their faces were too simple to be expressive, but each slumped their little shoulders or threw their arms into the air or banged their heads against the cabinet walls in frustration at having to see her again. Dizzy wouldn't let them go until she got what she wanted.

She held up the black card.

"This symbol mean anything to any of you?"

The dolls leaned forward to inspect the card, exchanged glances, and then shook their heads at her.

Humph.

"What about the name Hagenti?"

III reached up to try and pull the cabinet door shut over them again but Dizzy slammed it back open and flicked the doll between the eyes.

"I thought so," she said. "You know where he is?"

II put his head in his hands while *I* gesticulated wildly. Dizzy imagined profanity-laden protests in that Old Tejas accent he had back when he was a man who could speak.

"Doesn't matter." Dizzy waved her hand. "You're going to find Tomas Pascal for me."

II drew his arm across his throat.

"*Find*, not kill. I have questions. His answers will lead me to Hagenti, and—if you're lucky—that will lead to your release."

The dolls conferred in silence before hopping down from their shelves in resignation. One by one, they hopped out of the open window to the fire escape, *I* turning back long enough to give her something like a middle finger before disappearing from view. They'd done this plenty of times before. All she had to do was wait. In the meantime, she downed her newest glass of bourbon and began preparing the water to wash her floors.

The circumstances were not ideal. She had, after all, begun the day with a demon in her bedroom and she'd choke on all the herb that needed to be burned to cleanse *that* type of presence from the flat. But a thick undead aura had accumulated here, hanging like static in the air, so a little procedure was better than none.

She started in the kitchen and scrubbed black salt and bergamot spirit water in circles into the wooden floors. For hours, she tried to move her mind toward peace so it would manifest when her cleaning was done, but she couldn't shake thoughts of the violence she'd visit on Tommy when she found him. Her lips moved in their mantra, banishing all lingering malevolent spirits from this place, but thoughts of Carmen stuck in her mind as an ill she didn't truly want gone. She scrubbed the adjoining rooms harder and tried to replace images of Carmen with Lonnie and then images of Lonnie with nothing at all.

By the time she was done, she was eight fingers into a new bourbon bottle and it was not yet noon. She rested against the wall in her bedroom as sunlight began to work its way through the breaking clouds. Rain still dripped from the gutters and onto the fire escape but the gray sky beyond it was edged in gold that leaked unwelcome into the room.

She was in no hurry to dismiss the mirage of Lonnie she daydreamed onto the bed. It was some blend of memories Dizzy had from sitting on the floor of their apartment on the other side of the city. Lonnie sat there, resplendent in some slouchy t-shirt, mouthing the words of some long-forgotten conversation while she framed another one of Dizzy's show posters. She glanced up, a question reflected in her eyes. Whatever Dizzy's response had been made her laugh.

Dizzy smiled, too. Then she blinked and the room dimmed again. The phantom was gone.

Her guitar in its case stood like a shadow beside the altar. She tapped out the rhythm of a song on her thigh for a long while before reaching for it. It had gotten to the point where the apple-red skin of the instrument seemed lurid and accusing against the perpetual cloud of her life. And in the face of what could certainly be another dead end, another failure to see Lonnie's murderer repaid, she struggled with whether or not to grip it at all.

"What's the last song you played me?" said Lonnie's voice.

Dizzy looked up to see a memory of her again, standing by the window and staring down at her.

"Play that one."

If Lonnie's voice said to play, there wasn't a thing alive or dead could keep her still. She propped the guitar on her lap and her fingers floated the places they belonged. As she began to strum and pluck and rock, she marveled at how the thing was still immaculately tuned as if it'd been waiting for her after all. Her voice, on the other hand, came to her as if strained through gravel.

My love for you will never die...

It was some song much older than she was, retread in dive bars and desert saloons and what was left of the old juke joints but Lonnie loved her version so that's what she played. She found herself screaming the screaming parts with new anguish and knocking her beats on the wood veneer like it was a door to hell she wanted desperately to be let into if it meant the pain—the world—would just stop.

And when she cried her last note and stillness settled over the room again, she was left with the ache of her fingers and a stone in her chest. Outside, the traffic kept moving.

I T HAD BEEN years since she'd drawn the chalk seeing circle on her bedroom floor. The dolls had been gone all day, and it was time to check on them. The sun was down and the yellows, violets, and blues of San Guin's neon night had returned.

Dizzy was perhaps less sober than she should have been as she muttered her runes. A more devout witch would have been in this circle all day, praying for guidance or clarity until her knees were cut to bleeding on the hardwood floors or the ghosts returned, whichever came first. But over the years she'd discovered her power worked the same whether she gave thanks for it with every breath or none at all. She preferred efficiency to humility.

She centered herself in the circle and closed her eyes. When she opened them again, she was seeing through *I*'s eyes, watching a poker game through a dusty basement window. She checked the faces of every suited, drunken man present and found none of them were Tommy or any of the brujos she recognized. She closed her eyes again and reopened them inside *II* staring upskirt beneath the stairs of some side-street brothel. She groaned, and with a swipe of her hand, the doll's body slammed into a wall.

Presumably, he'd gotten the point.

When she opened her eyes in *III*, she was in an alley, dark and barren but for a blue-white light over an otherwise unremarkable door in a brick wall. Nothing happened for nearly a full minute. She was about to jog his memory for him when none other than Tommy walked into her field of vision. He approached the door and something from his pocket. A key, perhaps. A high-pitched beep suggested a key card. He disappeared inside. *III* looked around for landmarks and Dizzy recognized a cluster of billboards off an adjacent street high overhead.

Excited, she closed her eyes again, and opened them in her own body just long enough to step outside the circle before she was swept off her feet, banged into her wall and held there by a ringed skeleton hand.

"Well, if it ain't Dizzy 'I Don't Know When to Quit' Carter," said the undead witch, Uma. If deadwalkers had covens, Uma'd have been a High Priestess. She taught Dizzy everything she knew before dropping dead of a gunshot wound at a blackjack game about a decade ago. What was left of her skin stretched smooth over the bones of her face. There was still a little brown to it. The one indomitable mole once high on her cheek had migrated southward toward her neck but tattooed eyeliner still rimmed her white eyes. And she still knew how to dress. All things considered, the old girl looked good.

"Uma, darlin', how are you?" Dizzy choked.

"Better than you from the smell of things, and I'm dead. What are you now? 70, 80% brown liquor?" Uma grinned, revealing one of her gold teeth was still intact.

"62?"

"And still so *funny*. Well I'll tell ya Dizzy girl, I wish your comedy was why I'm here."

"Yeah, I thought not. Can you put me down maybe, and we can talk?" Dizzy asked. For all her own formidability, she knew better than to raise a hand to the dead, least of all one who had been like a mother to her in a few ways.

"I think we're fine where we are," Uma purred. "See you owe the dead a debt and I come to collect. You got them talking shit about me because the girl I raised don't pay what she owe and I gotta tell ya, I'm feeling real disrespected on both sides of this line."

"The ghosts are not here right now."

"Oh I know. I see you was just talking to 'em. So we gon' wait til they get here and I'ma collect the shit out of *all* y'all at the same time. How that sound?"

"It's not my time, Uma. You know that."

"You *say* that, but..." Uma's voice dropped to an ethereal growl and her hand started to squeeze vice-like around Dizzy's throat.

"What if I can deliver Lonnie's soul, too? And her murderer?"

"See that's what I'm talking about, Dizzy. We gon' talk about these games you play when we get home..."

"Uma, I'm serious." Dizzy's eyes ached but she looked as sternly as she could through them. "That's what I was just talking to the ghosts about. A man named Tomas Pascal is in league with some demon Hagenti and this guy the Magician. They knew Lonnie and I'm not sure but I can feel it in my bones they did something to her. *They did something.*"

She didn't mean to croak that last bit out. It wasn't as if crying would help her here but a tear squeezed out anyway. Lonnie did not die peacefully. She was tortured. Her tongue cut out and her mouth sewn shut elsewhere. These men did at least part of that to her and Dizzy felt like her heart was being ripped from her chest every time she thought about it.

Uma froze and inspected Dizzy for lies but her hand stayed where it was. At least it was no longer squeezing.

"I ain't teach you nothing about chanting down no demons. How you figure you might pull that off?"

"You know me. You know I'll figure it out. It was you who got me on hell's bad side in the first place, remember? So any delays are on you."

Uma chuckled. "Mm-hmm. That Madam probably gassed you up. What if you wrong?"

"I'm not." Dizzy replied with all the confidence she could muster with her feet dangling in the air. "You tell the dead they can have the ghosts, Lonnie, Tommy, the Magician, even me if they want when this is over but I have to see it through, Uma. Time's wasting and you have to let me go. I have to go *right now.*"

After what felt like forever, Uma relaxed her grip on Dizzy's throat.

"The only reason I don't drag you to hell is because I loved Lonnie, too," she said to the doubled-over Dizzy. "But I tell you what: you find this demon, you call us. Brawlin' your way out of this one will get you killed."

"What do you know about trapping demons?" Dizzy groaned.

"Don't you worry about that. And don't make me come back here, either."

"People keep saying that…" She stood back upright long enough to see Uma walk into a wall and disappear into wisps of black smoke.

The list of things she'd only half done to keep these sorts of visits from occurring ran on a ticker tape in her head as she grabbed her keys, gun, and phone and hurried out the door.

Nightlife traffic wasn't nearly as thick on the weekdays, so she made it to her destination beneath the cluster of billboards in fifteen minutes instead of forty. From there, she circled blocks in the vicinity of where *III* had been, which took considerably longer. Her mouth was still dry from the day's bourbon but few things were more sobering on the mind than a visit from Uma. She caught the bruises on her throat from where the woman had held her in the rearview mirror. Just when her head started pounding, she turned down a block of closed-up shops and rolled past an alley with a blue-white light.

She parked and checked the skyline for the right angle on that cluster of billboards to make sure she was in the right place. The door was on the side of a dark building with warehouse windows on its face and a HEATING'S TECH sign on its roof. She knew the company well. Its alarm systems dominated the city but this building appeared dilapidated at best. She checked her corners before heading down the alley, hoping Tommy was still behind the door.

The dolls dropped from a fire escape where they'd been waiting for her.

"Has he left yet?" she asked quietly.

The dolls shook their heads.

Relieved, she tugged on the door. Locked, of course. She'd have missed the thin magnetic strip beside the handle if she hadn't seen Tommy use it. She tapped the black card against it, the beep sounded, and the door released.

The card back in her pocket, she pulled her gun and stepped into the dark, the dolls following close behind her.

She stood on a mesh metal walkway in a hall with painted cinderblock walls and little else. The only light came from the red exit sign over her head. The walkway angled off into stairs going upward forever but only downward for a story or two. She listened for any sound that might tell her which direction to head first.

There were voices, warbled and indistinct as if they came from a television or radio somewhere. She peered over the railing and caught a thin strip of blue light beneath another door on the floor below.

She moved quickly and silently down the stairs and pressed her ear to the door until she was certain the TV behind it had been abandoned and she wasn't about to be surprised.

"Stay here," she whispered to the dolls as she turned the knob and opened the door slightly. The business end of her gun got the first glimpse into the room. As she peered in cautiously behind it, her eyes adjusted to the blue-white light of hundreds of tiny screens that covered the walls inside it.

"The fuck…" she muttered as she emerged fully inside. No one was there, not now anyway, but an empty swivel chair and a sweaty Big Gulp near a keyboard indicated that might not last long.

Each screen in the neverending grid was about the size of a hand, but these weren't television channels. As Dizzy inspected them, she found entirely regular people walking along sidewalks and through the hallways of their own homes. They ordered at drive-thru windows and stumbled out of bars and after-hours affairs at the office. They folded laundry and snuck cigarettes on balconies and tucked in their children before resuming arguments with spouses in the kitchen.

Cameras?

The surveillance situation in San Guin was layered.

Most cameras were privately owned by the business owners who had something to protect; the detection and deterrent settings depended on what manner of being they wanted to detect or deter. But there wasn't a network. There was barely a central anything, apart from power and light. And these were placements and angles no one with a security concern would care about. From what she could tell, no one knew they were there.

Bits of white tape sectioned off cameras monitoring parts of the city like a giant video map. She followed the tape toward her own address and sighed in relief that the closest cameras overlooked the Thai restaurant and a few of the downstairs shops.

She looked for the Rising Sun's district and found only its exterior as part of a long shot of its street.

And then she looked for the west side apartment she'd shared with Lonnie. Rosetta Drive wasn't exactly tree-lined but it was clean and calmer than most other parts of the city. The shadows there were different, illuminated by more street lamps and the diffused glow of bedroom windows than neon signs and traffic signals. Between her gigs and Lonnie's newly-blossoming acting career, they could afford the studio apartment atop the pink sandstone building at the top of the street. The staggered balconies spiraled upward like leaves.

She found the cameras that monitored its entrance, the elevator with its cracked marble floor, bare-board hallways. It was hard to distinguish their old home from the others with none of the familiar trappings. But she recognized the view through their old balcony door.

Before the creeping rage overtook her body, she heard a faint clattering in the direction of a narrow corridor on the far side of the room and her gun went back up. She held her breath and waited for a threat to emerge, but none did immediately. She pressed herself against the wall beside the opening and listened as Tomas's heavy footsteps drew nearer.

He spotted her as he stepped into the room, a startled question developing in his eyes before he realized Dizzy's gun was drawn and aimed at his chest.

"Cart—whoa!" he yelled and slapped her hand away in a panic. The gun went off, firing into a monitor behind him. He banged her hand into the wall until she dropped it and then backhanded her across the face. Dizzy recovered in time to take a short breath before his giant fists were around her neck, slamming her into a display panel and squeezing so hard she spit.

"What are you *doing*?" He shook her as if she could answer.

Ordinarily now would have been a good time for some eye gouging, clawing, anything really to get free, but Tommy's reach vastly outmatched Dizzy's. She brought her fists down on his forearms with all the force she could muster to get his elbows to buckle and when she was within reach, boxed his ears.

Tommy roared as he released her and dropped to his knees. Dizzy scrambled for the gun and caught him one good time across the face with it, sending a small spray of his blood against a control panel.

"Stay down," she heaved and gulped, her fury still too fresh to register the pain she'd undoubtedly feel in the morning.

Tommy nodded and gestured time out, pulling himself into the swivel chair. "Jesus, Carter," he panted. "If this is about the Sun, tell them I got the point."

"Tell me where *here* is. What is all this?"

"You a cop now?" he asked, pulling a cigarette from its crushed case and lighting it.

"I'm an impatient woman with a gun and a bad fucking headache," Dizzy growled.

He nodded slowly and spit the blood accumulating in his mouth onto the concrete floor. "They didn't tell you I'm protected? I can't be killed."

Dizzy flicked the black card at him. "Yeah I heard about your little brand," she said. She shot him in his foot and he doubled over, screaming obscenities through clenched teeth in three languages.

"I'll settle for that. What is this place?"

"It's a God's Eye monitoring system for Heating's Tech Surveillance and Security," he spat. "I don't know what it's for, I just run it. Been here eight years, shut down a few years ago but I just got orders a couple months back to get it going again."

Dizzy moved back toward the shot of her old apartment. "So all this was functional during the Fallen Angel murders. Were y'all much help with those investigations?"

Tommy glared up at her but said nothing.

"Lonnie Baxter lived right here," she said, tapping the screen. "I know because I lived there with her. Her tongue was cut out, her mouth sewn shut, and then her spine was snapped in half when she was dropped onto our neighbor's balcony. So am I taxing *you* or someone else for that?"

"You're gonna have to shoot me again," he muttered, exhaling smoke through his nose.

Dizzy strode over and pressed the gun against his temple. The muzzle was still hot and the blood and sweat sizzled a bit on his head. "Again, I don't have a lot of time," she said calmly. "So, this might not kill you but we can find out together what it *does* do…"

Tommy winced at the pain and spit again before relenting.

"Mr. Heating, alright? Presidente Hagenti. He used the camera system to find his targets. Called them muses."

"Then what?"

Tommy screwed up his face and shrugged. "Then, you know, they got hunted down, grabbed, stashed."

"Who did the hunting?"

He was reluctant to answer. She shot him in the knee.

"*Fuck! We did!*" he howled. "He did everything else. I don't know why he did all that mouth-sewing shit but he flies in his other form and dropped those people because he said it was art. It's fucked up but that's what he said."

Dizzy's head spun. All these years and the lead she needed had been under her nose or down the hall bedding a friend and she hadn't seen it. She wanted to kill him. She wanted to scream. Neither of these things would be productive in the moment. "So you watched us? You knew who I was when we met in that alley and you let me leave you alive?" Dizzy scoffed. "Was it you? Did you grab Lonnie?"

Tommy shook his head pitifully. "Look, your girl wasn't supposed to go like that. She was tough. She escaped and made it back to your spot but he found her. It was an accident when she fell."

"*Was it you?*"

"Yes and no," he said in a frantic stammer. "We...are legion. We take his mark, we do what we're told, and nothing living can kill us. So did I touch her? No. But if one of the legion did, so did I."

"You said you were ordered to start this back up again. Why? He in town? About to get going again?"

"I swear I don't know what he wants with it but he's back in San Guin as of a few weeks ago. There's a...a gallery thing he's opening on the mezzanine of the Gōrudo Theater. Vintage District, next Wednesday night. If you can get in, you can take all this up with him."

Dizzy nodded, thinking as she stared vacantly at the scenes in the tiny screens around her. The copper smell of Tommy's blood invaded her nose. Someone had just come home in the scene of her old apartment. A young father carried a sleeping toddler past the camera and gently placed his keys on the kitchen counter. Fatigue suddenly weighed heavily on her. Fatigue or sadness.

"You said nothing living could kill you?" she muttered. Tired, she walked back to the door and opened it again. "Gentlemen," she called and stepped back so the three dolls waiting in the stairwell could enter.

Tommy squinted as if certain he wasn't seeing them correctly. They were not puppets. There were no strings.

"These men are dead," Dizzy declared.

"What is this?" Tommy frowned. Despite himself, he made attempts to stand and inch backward.

"Tommy here's our first big break in years, which means you're all that much closer to glory," she told the dolls. "Finish him. I'll be in the car."

One by one, the dolls began to splinter as if bursting out of themselves, the bits of them linking end to end and blistering until each was transformed into a 7-foot-tall monster of fine spikes limbering up and sneering down at Tomas.

"Dizzy, I told you I didn't touch your girl!" he said, terror getting the best of him as the dolls stalked forward.

"I know, but you're legion. If you feel this, so will they," said Dizzy. She stepped beyond the door and closed it softly behind her. His screams followed her up the stairs.

IZZY SAT IN the car outside her apartment scrolling through internet photos of the demon who owned San Guin's energy infrastructure. Niles Heating—Hagenti; the laziness of it made her want to spit knowing how clever he must have thought it was—towered over most other people in the photos with him. He was a giant with a disgusting amiability about his facial expressions. He appeared at ribbon cuttings and symposiums and photographed so dark in stylish, heroic profiles where he stood among a hundred bright, bare bulbs that one could be forgiven for thinking there was a person-shaped void burned into the image.

She wondered how long he'd been in San Guin, how long it took to make himself king and what the endgame was. Carmen said something about the balance shifting. Demons were becoming more interested in the city. There was already a tenuous balance of life and un-life here. More demons could only mean trouble.

More than one person had told her that wasn't her business, though. For now, she could believe them. What she needed was Lonnie back. And for that to happen, she needed a way to dispatch a demon.

"Wait here," she told the dolls in her back seat. *II* climbed up by the rear window to make a show of bashing his tiny head against the glass as she exited the car.

Instead of going inside, she crossed over to Mark Street, past the pocket bars and street vendors to the alley behind the noodle shop where she knew the Colorman's Disciples were undoubtedly up to something they shouldn't have been up to. These were thieves and graffiti artists casually known as Krylon Kids. And they were as adept as rats at getting into places you didn't want them to go.

Dizzy would have to avoid cameras. There was no telling what would become of the God's Eye system once whatever remained of Tommy was discovered. And her brand of magic required time and concentration. There would be no brawling with a bull. She had to set the stage herself.

She wound through the typical scenes of late-night debauchery, past silhouettes of the casual dead in their enjoyment of watching life, and into a hazy, bass-thumping dark behind the noodle shop. An all-consuming mural of the Krylon King himself occupied the rear wall of an apartment building on the opposite side of the alley, rendered in high definition.

The Colorman on the wall sat cross-legged, dapper in a teal blue suit, twelve arms fanned around him like peacock feathers, each ending in a dark brown hand pointing in this or that direction. His bed was stark white clouds crisply lined in cerise no. 45 and the gold piled along his neck and wrists glinted in metallic goldenrod.

The rest of the long block wall was painted in tessellated starbursts like radiated tortoise shells. It was an improvement if you didn't mind the company. The Disciples threw up these murals wherever the Colorman needed eyes. They became doorways the kids could use like portals throughout the city to flee police after this or that criminal or mischievous enterprise.

Dizzy paused in rounding the corner in time to see three people come crashing through the Colorman's door. They were bundles of dark clothing, the only color flashing on the bottom of their sneakers. Each was panting and stumbling and carrying backpacks full of who-knows-what as they skidded to a stop before smashing into the next wall and pivoting to take off past her toward the street.

Close on their heels, another form skidded through the door. This one, a hellhound, the vantablack, musclebound pups kept as pets by the heads of the global gangs.

Dizzy blinked surprise, remaining stock still in the corner by a dumpster. What you didn't want was a hellhound to find you interesting.

This one was dotted with lime green handprints and seemed more than a little pissed off about it. It darted off after them. Screams and angry car horns were added to the sounds of Front Street, pierced by the dog's deep and chilling bark.

A whistle.

Dizzy turned back to the mural and the alleyway. The Colorman's eyes flicked in Dizzy's direction.

Six kids in various states of obscured identity halted in the shaking of their spray paint cans and looked at her.

"You lost?" one of the masked kids called from atop a fire escape.

"Not at all," Dizzy called back. She gave the Colorman a lazy salute so as not to seem rude. "Who here can I talk to about a job?"

A girl on the ground with her hair in lime streaked cornrows sauntered over and lifted her gas mask. "Noodle spot's got applications. You look like you could wait a good table." She smirked.

"No, I need to hire you. I need a gateway into the Gōrudo Theatre in the next couple days. You know it?"

"We don't know what you're talking about." She sniffed dismissively. Two of her friends began walking over for support.

"I'm not a cop. You know this man?" Dizzy showed the girl a picture of Niles Heating standing beneath a backlit sign for Heating Power & Light.

The girl glanced back at her friends and then at Dizzy as if to ask if she was crazy. "Sure, we know him."

"Then you know he's loaded. You might have even done some work for him in the past. I heard he has a thing for stolen art."

"Like I said, we don't kno—"

"I don't care. You get me into the Gōrudo, you get access to all of his shit and you'll get to it before one of the global gangs does."

"How?" asked one of the kids who'd just joined them. "You gonna take him out?"

"I don't know what you're talking about," Dizzy replied with a shrug, shoving her phone back into her pocket. "So?"

The leader was silent for a second, wanting to appear thoughtful and measured in front of an adult. Dizzy allowed the performance.

"I'll talk to the boss," she said finally.

"Good. I'll be back here the night after tomorrow." Dizzy winked at the Colorman's mural and his eyes returned to their neutral position.

She nodded at N in her stall on the way home. For once, she didn't feel the need for a drink.

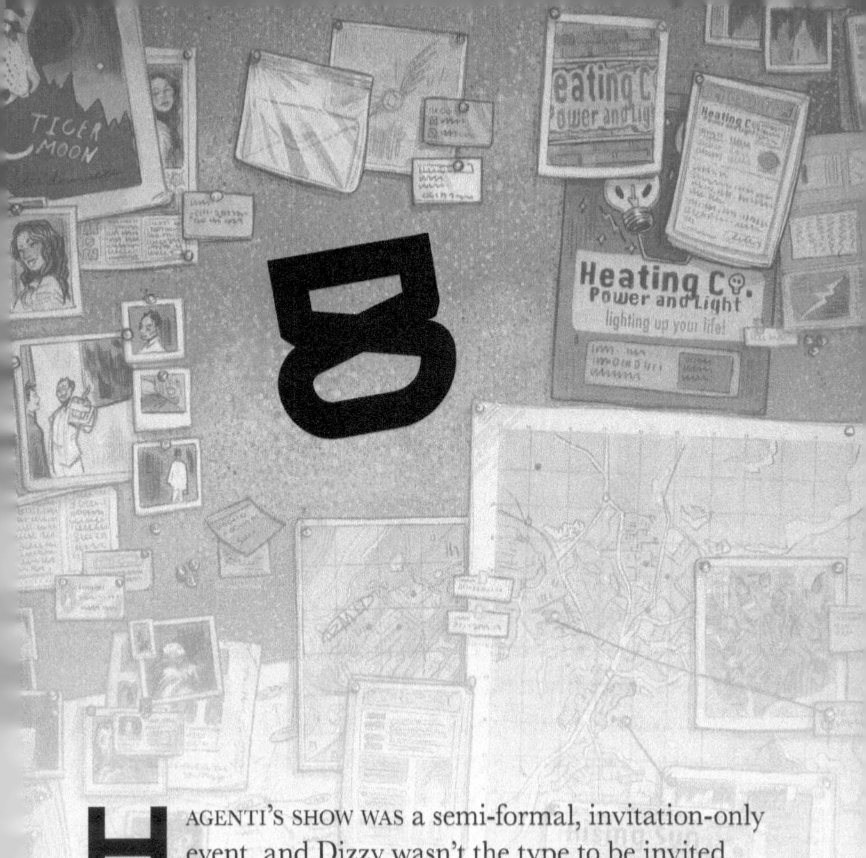

8

H AGENTI'S SHOW WAS a semi-formal, invitation-only event, and Dizzy wasn't the type to be invited anywhere. Carmen, on the other hand, could charm her way into any building that wasn't a church; Dizzy asked for her help getting in and she obliged.

She parked outside the Rising Sun, chewing too hard on flavorless gum and idly itching the cut in her palm she'd used to make more bloodstones. Her other hand was still stained with the paint mark that granted her passage through the Colorman's gateway.

She turned over the plan in her mind. There was no mention in the news, not about Tomas or what was left of him in that basement. If he was still there, still rotting, it didn't matter much to her. But it was more likely he'd failed to check in and someone more interesting than San Guin's finest went looking for him and cleaned up what they found.

In any case, she might just be on someone's radar now. She would have one chance—her last chance—to finish this.

Carmen emerged from the wrought-iron doors in a tempting blue dress something like the devil might wear. Dizzy got out in her own shirtsleeves and suspenders and moved around to open the passenger-side door for her.

"My, my, my Dizzy Carter. Do they still say chivalry is dead?" Carmen smiled.

"I'm not a *complete* animal." Dizzy kissed her gently. "Now you can't say I never take you anywhere."

"Ha!" Carmen cackled as she settled into the car and Dizzy closed the door.

"Ash coming?" Dizzy asked as she started the engine.

"She's already there. How are you? You alright?"

"Just hot," said Dizzy, not exactly lying. "You know how long it's been since I've worn a tie?"

The Vintage District was sort of an artisan's refuge, a few blocks of buildings, workshops, and warehouses that hadn't been renovated in decades, just adapted because nothing said "I'm an artist" like bare brick and living in old-world squalor. Dizzy knew it well. Her music flourished here.

The Gōrudo Theatre was undoubtedly the jewel of the place with its scalloped gold facade and stained glass dome rising high on a block of experimental art galleries and low-key 24-hour brunch spots. It was once a great operatic venue, but opera was long dead. She'd snuck inside to poke around and rehearse in its acoustic environment growing up. But tonight was the first time Dizzy had ever seen the building alive with light.

Dizzy parked across the street in front of a bare brick diner that smelled of brunch. The Theatre offered valet service, but again, no one drove stick anymore.

"That smells amazing," Carmen mused as they crossed the street. "When this is done, I could see this being appropriate for a proper date if you're looking for ideas."

"Noted," Dizzy replied, putting on her jacket. Her attention was on the people entering the building, on the people wandering happily just inside the gallery doors and beyond them to the off-limits theatre floor she would need access to later. It was one thing to get up there with a skeleton crew on the grounds. Now that the place was swarming with people—any number of whom could be part of the Legions—things seemed a bit more complicated.

Carmen got them checked off with the doorman and they made their way inside. The trendy art-lovers-of-influence mingled on the polished marble floors of the lobby, drinking champagne and taking in the near ancient architecture of the interior. Chandeliers of colored crystal hung massive from the vaulted ceiling and dramatic fabric tapestries of winged muses and creatures in noh masks lined the walls. From cracked balustrades to iridescent threads braided into silk drapes, everything was somehow accented in gold.

The crimson-carpeted grand staircase to the theatre floor was blocked by velvet ropes and the sorts of bored men whose one job it was to keep drunken party-goers from sneaking off to it. They watched Dizzy. Or rather they watched Carmen—the men did, anyway.

"You know you don't have to stay," Dizzy said as they made their way to the showroom.

"Relax. I'm *supposed* to be a distraction, remember?" Carmen assured her, and plucked a champagne glass from a gobsmacked caterer's tray.

Dizzy hated to admit Carmen was right almost as much as she hated the idea of using her this way. But cameras were everywhere and she needed Carmen's allure to distract them when she separated Mr. Heating from his magician.

They weaved their way through colorful sculptures of blown glass on pedestals in the gallery, some with items like car keys and cotton hearts with needles in them suspended at their centers. The happy faces and the aloof ones of art cynics equally had no idea they were here on the invitation of a murderer. And if they did, they didn't show it bothered them any.

Twenty minutes into the search, Dizzy began to scowl.

"So what do I call you now?" Carmen finally asked to the back of the tall, dark man in what had to be a vantablack suit. "Is it Mr. Heating now or is Gen still good?"

He turned to reveal a handsome and neatly-bearded face, twinkling eyes and a plain gold ring in his nose. His teeth were a startling white as he smiled down at them.

"Carmen," he greeted her in an impressive baritone, took her hand, and kissed it. "You can call me whatever you'd like."

"Heard you were in town and I couldn't stay away. This is Desdemona, my…paramour," she purred. Dizzy could tell by the cool mischief in her eyes that she enjoyed the little dig.

"Dizzy is fine," she said, inspecting Hagenti's expression for any hint that he recognized her from his surveillance of Lonnie's life.

"Welcome, Dizzy," he said, smiling in a disarmingly warm way. Dizzy's jaw clenched as she thought about this same charm being used to lure Lonnie. She stifled her rage for now.

The shorter man beside him had turned around as well. He was older, or at least human enough to exhibit age. The skin of his face seemed irritated, like he'd been sunburned and then piled on makeup to hide it. He was decidedly less attractive but the smirk resting on his leathery face suggested he didn't know it.

The man in white.

"I don't believe I've had the pleasure," the man said in a sing-song voice as he shook Carmen's hand. "I'm Walter. Old friend of Mr. Heating."

"Interesting. I thought I knew all of his old friends," Carmen purred. Her lidded gaze flickered over him as if he wasn't really there.

"Not quite," Walter simpered, still staring at Dizzy. No one else seemed to notice he hadn't offered her his hand. Just as well. She'd have ripped it off.

"This is quite a show, Gen," Carmen said.

"Well, what you walked through were all pieces commissioned from artisans I've met through my travels. Truly inspiring human beings with such uniqueness to their processes I just had to have them. *These* are mine." He gestured toward one long wall where glittering, glistening, jewel-toned broken glass embedded in eight hanging canvases hung as if bottles had been thrown at them and stayed where they shattered beautifully.

Dizzy's eye twitched. Eight canvases of shattered glass. Eight crime scenes of shattered people. Which of these was meant to be Lonnie?

"Brilliant, isn't it?" Walter's eyes sparked as the four of them walked among the works. "Mr. Heating's eye for the beauty in unmade things is unmatched in my experience."

"So much is made to serve such small purpose," Mr. Heating mused. "These glass bottles were vessels for other things deemed more important than the vessels themselves. It was only by taking them apart—even in such a violent way—that they were elevated to something more than debris."

Carmen and Dizzy glanced at each other as if asking silently if he meant to be this on-the-nose with his ravings. They stopped in front of a canvas of sunny orange glass. Under this light and from the right angle it did seem to spiral into a pattern of splayed limbs. Like an angel with a broken back.

"I don't see it," Dizzy said flatly. Mr. Heating's smile faltered a moment but Walter's persisted.

"I'm sorry," Mr. Heating scoffed. "What do you mean you don't see it?"

Dizzy fought to keep her eyebrow from raising and shrugged instead. "Looks like a tantrum to me. Something a toddler would do if you kept glass around him. And if you don't mind some criticism…"

"Why would I mind?" he asked quickly, defensively, his forced smile twitching on his lips.

"Well you've taken something perfectly whole and, as you said, purposeful, that in its intact state could have lived a hundred lives as a vessel for other things," Dizzy said smoothly. "And instead of appreciating its beautiful parts when whole, you shattered it. Destroyed it. And reduced it to something only good for looking at. In any other context, this is a mess of pieces for someone else to pick up, try and salvage or just throw away."

She knew perfectly well the screws she was twisting. Carmen gave her a look that implied she should reel it in while Mr. Heating tutted and sputtered for something to say.

"Well, not all art is for everyone," Walter volunteered, and passed around champagne flutes from a passing tray.

Dizzy downed hers almost immediately as Carmen linked arms with the other demon and changed the subject.

There was no way Walter wasn't the magician, she thought. He had all the insufferable entitlement of someone who'd attached himself to immortality by any means necessary. And he knew her in a way that Hagenti—in all his focus on the art and none of the logistics—did not. She didn't put it past him to have orchestrated the grabbing of victims for his master to transform.

Walter excused himself from their group and headed up a short flight of stairs on the far side of the exhibit to the restroom. Dizzy whispered in Carmen's ear that it was time to move.

She followed Walter's path, looking back to make sure Carmen excused herself from Mr. Heating as they'd discussed. Things were going to get sticky and there was no way to know what would happen once the magician died. It was best to plan for havoc.

A uniformed attendant leaning against a counter just inside the door winked at Dizzy. It took her a moment to realize the attendant was Ash looking more like a working-class drag king than her usually made-up self. Beside her on the counter was the small wooden box Dizzy had handed over earlier in the day, containing her dolls.

Ash tapped the box and went to take her leave. "Still two ladies in here. Should be out soon," she said quietly.

Dizzy nodded and took the box from her. She waited in the powder room, an antechamber to the toilets furnished with mirrors and striped couches, for the two other women to leave before locking the door behind them. Walter was washing his hands as she emerged from the doorway.

He only glanced up. "Miss Baxter would have been Mr. Heating's finest piece," he cooed. "He was so taken with her. Her beauty. Her spirit. But you know all about that, don't you? It's that tenacity of hers we underestimated. Mr. Heating was disappointed to lose her. We drugged all of them so they felt no pain by the end. Funny how she didn't go to the police. But in her delirium, all she was looking for was you."

He took a beat to dry his hands and found no kindness or even interest in Dizzy's face as she undid her jacket and hung it on a stall door.

"I saw what happened to Mr. Pascal. I'll admit I'm surprised to see you again," he shouted over the dryer. "I'd say it's a small world but I suppose this isn't an accident on your part. What are you here for? To turn us in? Finally get some *justice*?"

"Where is Lonnie?" Dizzy asked, rolling her sleeves.

He stared at her a moment, frowning for the first time that night. "I don't understand. She's dead, dear. Quite dead. *Six years* dead."

"Not quite, no," Dizzy said, irritation mounting in her voice. "You and the bull have her ghost and I want it back."

"Aren't we the astute little witch."

"Smarmy fuck…"

"My dear I'm afraid you are out of your depth here," he said. His voice dripped with condescension. "A demon's got nothing to do with the dead."

Dizzy flipped the latch on the box and placed the dolls at her feet.

"One last time, boys," she sighed and they began to grow into her monsters. She was immune to Walter's gaze now. A dozen men had all had the same horrified expressions when presented with her dolls. Some of them pleaded automatically. Others played hard to get. The magician seemed inclined to the latter but his calm facade was cracked. That, too, happened sometimes.

"Hold him still," she commanded, and the hulking splinter creatures dashed to pin him hard to the wall. Their razor-thin spines sliced into the sleeves of his suit and the collar of his shirt and thin blood lines appeared in the cuts. He was looking much more horrified now, staring into their hollow faces instead of at Dizzy. She approached and pressed her thumbs to the inner corners of his eyes and began reciting her runes again.

Both their eyes went black and the searing heat of her touch made the magician scream as she read his sight for the last time he'd seen Lonnie. One of the dolls clapped a hand over his mouth. She soared back through six years of his sight until she recognized Lonnie's fleeing form in the white dress, the struggle in the apartment, and finally her lying back-broken over the railing and gasping for breath. Walter took her soul into his mouth and breathed it into a large, gold coin, something like a Spanish doubloon with a torch on its tails-side.

Dizzy released him and searched his pockets while he moaned there, blinded and bleeding. She found it, turning out his inner jacket pockets and nearly sobbed when she could feel the energy coming off it. It could easily have been another ghost he'd stolen from someone else but she knew this one was Lonnie. And it hadn't been Hagenti who dropped her, though it was certainly the demon's fault. It was Walter.

She stepped away, running her fingers along its worn surfaces before stashing it in her trouser pocket and digging out a set of brass knuckles.

He only cried out once, the first time she hit him. After that, sounds like words or prayers began to tumble with the spittle from his lips as she struck him until all the bones in his face were broken or burned beneath swollen flesh. She felt keenly the moment he died, like a rush of warm wind as the ghosts let his body slump to the restroom floor.

Almost immediately, something like a blast rocked the room, and outside she heard screams and shattered glass. She moved to the door but *III* held her by the wrist, an accusing "you promised" in his gestures toward the other dolls.

"Yes, fine," she said, impatient. A snap of her fingers and the monsters reverted to idle dolls on the floor around the dead magician, their ghosts fleeing past her in their own gusts of air.

The gallery floor was a chaos of frantic people half-blinded by projectile glass and dropped chandeliers trying to navigate the colorful shard pools covering the floor. At their center, a bull-man in a vantablack suit roared in pain or embarrassment, it was hard to tell which. Without the magician, Hagenti couldn't hold his form. She was glad Carmen and Ash were out of there.

Dizzy skirted the main floor, sticking to the elevated walkway that ringed the room on the way to the freight elevator tucked behind heavy crushed-velvet curtains. She moved quickly, noticing that Hagenti had calmed and began sniffing the air around him angling in her direction.

"Which of you's the witch?" he demanded in a hellish growl as people scattered around him.

Dizzy ducked behind the curtains just as his eyes met hers and she mashed the UP button rapidly until the doors opened. The panic sounds died away and she was left with the hum of the elevator and her own subsiding adrenaline. The doors opened and she was in a backstage area of the auditorium illuminated scarcely by work lights. Drapes and snares of rope cast shadows on sledgehammered walls and the old wood of the floorboards groaned beneath her feet.

She made her way to centerstage where screams and sirens echoed beyond the theatre doors. The balconies were dark. Work lights edged the main floor, bright enough to see the Japanese damask wallpaper hanging torn and peeling from where the walls had warped over decades of sweltering heat.

Three thousand empty scarlet seats. She'd dreamed once of playing this room and having every one of them filled. A large block of the velvet center seats and carpeting had been removed as renovations started, stained as they were from where the vaulted, ornate ceiling had sprung leaks, so now the place only smelled slightly of mildew and more of just time.

It was in this open space her spiral of blood stones began.

In her preparations, she placed a lone stool at the center of a protection circle she'd drawn at center stage. What she hadn't done was leave the guitar she now found leaning against it.

A note attached read:

If you have time to kill. C.

Dizzy smirked and took a seat on the stool, lighting a caapi cigarette and looking out over the empty auditorium. The sounds from the floor below were increasingly violent. She exhaled smoke and flipped Lonnie's coin over in her blood-stained palm. In fact, much of her was stained with Walter's blood—her knuckles were budding bruises.

She remembered kissing Lonnie goodbye at the train station headed east to a shoot somewhere greener. She'd always preferred the scenic route. There was little glamor about her: jeans and a white t-shirt she'd pulled wrinkled from a pile of clean laundry. But her lipstick was plum colored and left Dizzy's stained something similar. Lonnie'd laughed as she tried to wipe it away.

A month later she'd kissed the same lips but they were pale and cold and supported by gauze and wire.

She brushed away an errant tear and huffed herself back together, tapping ash onto the stage. She picked up the guitar and let her fingers decide what to do with its strings.

I guess I keep a-gamblin'
Lots of booze and lots of ramblin'
It's easier than just waitin' around to die...

The auditorium acoustics were tinged with a crackle of small, falling debris. Guitar sounds resonated warmly in the empty room and her voice gradually found its strength again. She'd gotten through a verse and a half when the bull crashed the doors and stood huffing at the back of the room. Flashing blue and red lights at his back illuminated his hulking form as he stalked forward and entered the outer ring of her blood stone spiral.

"*You* are the witch?" he bellowed. "Do you have *any* idea how hard it is to find a magus in this era?"

Dizzy kept playing, only now she sang her incantations in the cadence of her song. She had nothing to say to him.

She inhaled the smoke and exhaled its tendrils until she could see them drawn into the spiral's center.

"Answer me, human!" Hagenti crashed through seats, batting them away like flies as he stalked toward the stage. Dizzy shut her eyes tight and chanted and prayed for the dead to take no more than what was theirs for the demon was her offering to them tonight.

"Oh, the masterpieces I will paint with a deadwalker's blood…" Hagenti roared. His voice was so close it startled Dizzy's eyes back open just in time to see him lunge for her—

Only to be held back by the edge of the circle.

He yanked and pulled as if against a chain tethering him to the center of the spiral but once the dead were inside it, none could leave.

Together we're gonna wait around and die

Dizzy sneered as a skeleton hand clasped her shoulder. Uma stood beside her, glowering down at the demon.

"What is this magic?" Hagenti demanded. His pitch black eyes were trained on her while the dead rose in the circle behind him. One. Two. Ten.

"You owe the dead a debt. We come to collect."

"The dead hold no dominion over demons," Hagenti grunted.

Uma laughed her three-voice laugh. "You say that, but…"

At once the twenty dead who'd sprouted from the ground around them descended on the demon.

"You should have stuck to your own," Uma told him as the dead slashed and dragged him back to the center of the spiral.

He fought back fiercely, even loosing his wings in great glittering obsidian arcs to sweep off their grasp. But the longer he stayed in the circle, the longer his essence was drained. There was no killing the dead and nothing but time subdued them.

"Dizzy girl, you ready?" Uma sighed like the dragging of demons was an everyday distraction from watching her stories.

Dizzy watched as Hagenti was pulled, beaten and cursing, into an unseen pit and figured she might as well be more dignified about her own departure. She stood and began to step out of her circle when Uma yanked her back.

"What are you doing? Chile, ain't nobody coming for you. I'm asking did you get what *you* come for? *Did you find Lonnie?*"

"Oh." Dizzy frowned, exhausted, and handed over the coin. "From our last conversation I assumed the dead wanted me."

Uma rolled it between her fingers. "Well you know they say assuming makes an *ass* out of *you*."

"That's not how that goes."

"Mm-hmm." Uma waved her off and snapped at her minions. "Y'all get Mr. President or whatever he calls himself under control? We are not long for this world and our hostess is going to have quite a time explaining all this to the law here in a minute." She jumped from the stage into the summoning circle where her bones began to smoke.

"What are you going to do with him?" Dizzy asked.

"Deliver him to evil. But that's his problem, not yours." Uma looked back at Dizzy. "Do you want to see her?" she asked.

For years the automatic answer to this question had been *yes*. Dizzy never imagined there would be a reason to pause. But here she was, tripping on her thoughts about what to say and what would come of it if Lonnie's ghost could say nothing back. She could apologize for not protecting her, for taking so long, for growing as comfortable as she was now with Carmen. But she wasn't prepared for her apologies to possibly go unaccepted. That might kill her.

"Would you believe I'm not ready?" she replied. Hagenti's cries died away, making the words seem louder, more toxic in the emptying room.

Uma nodded. "I do. She'll understand. The dead'll keep her safe 'til you're ready. But don't keep her waiting too long. I raised you better."

"Yeah you did."

In three steps, Uma's bones collapsed to dust within the circle and Dizzy was alone again with the dark and the caapi buzz in her skin. Flashlight strobes and authoritative voices from the busted-open door told her the police had arrived and would be stumbling upon her soon. Dazed and feeling sick, Dizzy grabbed her guitar and made her way uneasily back to the elevator. Her hands up, cops on the gallery level took her for another injured patron and shuffled her off through the exit toward medical attention.

The entire glass facade of the building was blown out and the shards twinkled in colors of emergency lights on the steps outside. The fresh midnight air breezed clear and cool and helped to steady the waves of nausea that swept through her in the post-caapi afterglow. Damn, she could use a drink.

She searched for Carmen among the terrified, confused faces of the injured around her. Her phone vibrated.

NEW MESSAGES
CARMEN 23:47 – BY THE CAR

Dizzy carved her way through the crowds to where Carmen waited, leaning against the passenger side door, her head cocked curiously and a smile playing about her lips.

"Good to see you're still alive. How'd it go?" Carmen smirked and made fruitless efforts to fix Dizzy's blood-smeared shirt.

"The guitar was a nice touch," Dizzy replied, appreciating for what felt like the first time the way Carmen's hands worried over her.

"I thought so. So did you——"

Dizzy kissed her first this time, deeply and propelled by something like relief and gratitude and a sea of things it didn't make sense just now to say with words. There was more to the sparks where their lips met than just Carmen's sweet venom. There would be time later to visit Maia and Emmanuelle, to help ease their heartache with the news and solidify any alliances against whatever hell intended next. All Dizzy needed right now was Carmen.

Heh, she thought, smiling. *Maybe the venom* does *work.*

"You're sticky," Carmen finally said, smiling against Dizzy's teeth.

"I know, right?" Dizzy laughed, delirious but also for the first time in a long time, happy.

"You need a shower."

"You sure? I was thinking this is the perfect time for that date. We're right here," Dizzy joked.

"No, you're a walking health code violation. You can make it up to me later."

"Suit yourself."

"Give me the keys. You're high as gas. I'll drive." Carmen headed to the driver's side.

"You can drive stick?" Dizzy raised an eyebrow and tossed her the keys.

"Dizzy, do you know how *old* I am?"

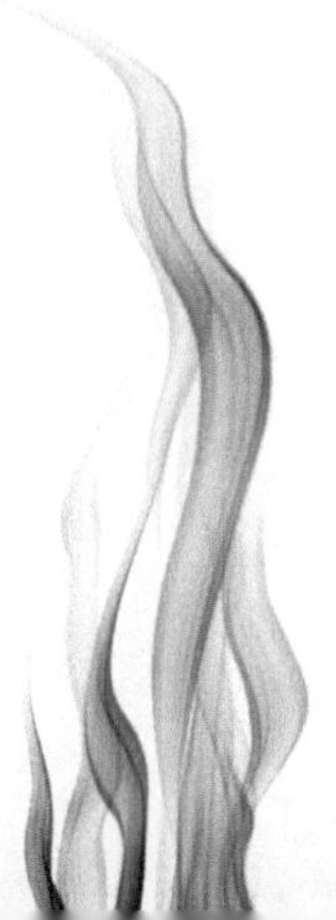

Heating Co.
Power and Light
Heating Co.
Power and Light
Heating Co.
Power and Light
lighting up your life!
REPORT
Rising Sun
Evening Star ★
HORROR AS MURDER

acknowledgments

Thank you…

...makers of paper and music, readers of books, speakers for the dead.

...Bean, Mochi, and Churro for being sustaining forces.

...dave, of course, and cover artist Shan Bennion.

...folks whose deadlines I frustrated by doing too much at once.

...everyone who ever asked "how are edits going" and tolerated whatever shrieking I did in response.

...Suzan, Marty, Jo for fitting the story into your lives.

My greatest thanks to Brent Lambert, my perfect reader, who was subjected to this story in a thousand iterations over the years and didn't let my intense and pointed questioning of his approval dim his enthusiasm for Dizzy and her shenanigans.

And Karintha, who knows why.

about the author

L. D. Lewis (she/her) is an editor, publisher, and Shirley Jackson award-nominated writer of speculative fiction. She served as a founding creator and Project Manager for the World Fantasy and Hugo Award-winning *FIYAH Literary Magazine*. Past lives include roles as the founding director of FIYAHCON and researcher for the LeVar Burton Reads podcast. She pays the bills as a literary nonprofit administrator. She is the author of novella *A Ruin of Shadows* (Dancing Star Press, 2018) and her published short fiction and poetry includes appearances in a number of online publications, Neon Hemlock anthologies, and Jordan Peele's *Out There Screaming*. Her debut novel *Year of the Mer* is forthcoming from Saga Press in 2026. She lives in Georgia on perpetual deadline with her partner, two cats, and an impressive LEGO build collection.

about the press

Neon Hemlock is a Washington, DC-based small press publishing speculative fiction, rad zines, and queer chapbooks. Publishers Weekly once called us "the apex of queer speculative fiction publishing" and we're still beaming. Learn more about us at neonhemlock.com and on social medias at @neonhemlock.